NIGHT MAGICK

Warlocks MacGregor®

MICHELLE M. PILLOW

MichellePillow.com

About Night Magick

Magic, Mischief and Kilts!

A modern-day Scottish paranormal romance by NYT Bestselling Author Michelle M. Pillow.

Maura might be new to the supernatural town of Green Vallis, but this isn't her first dance with the devil.

Half vampire, half human and full bar owner, Curtis Jefferson has spent a lifetime running from his vampiric ancestor. When the old nemesis finally catches up to him, it's only by a freak accident that he's not killed. But now the beautiful woman who saved his life has a target on her back.

As the new owner of the local motel, Maura

MacGregor doesn't have to live at the family mansion, affording her the ability to stay out of the limelight. She never thought the famed Warlock MacGregors' magickal troubles would manifest by way of a tall, dark, and hunky bar owner, but she doesn't get to make the rules. Fate does.

Warning: Contains yummy, hot, mischievous MacGregors who are almost certainly up to no good on their quest to find true love. And Uncle Raibeart.

Warlocks MacGregor® Series

SCOTTISH MAGICKAL WARLOCKS

Love Potions
Spellbound
Stirring Up Trouble
Cauldrons and Confessions
Spirits and Spells
Kisses and Curses
Magick and Mischief
A Dash of Destiny
Night Magick
A Streak of Lightning
Magickal Trouble

More Coming Soon

Visit www.MichellePillow.com for details.

Author Updates

Join the Reader Club Mailing List to stay informed about new books, sales, contests and preorders!

http://michellepillow.com/author-updates/

Note from the Author

The term "warlock" is a variation on the Old English word "waerloga" primarily used by the Scots. It meant traitor, monster, deceiver, or other variations. The MacGregors do not look at themselves as being what history has labeled their kind. To them, warlock means magick, family, and immortality. This book is not meant to be a portrayal of modern day witches or those who have such beliefs. The MacGregors are a magickal class all their own.

As with all my books, this is pure fantasy. In real life, please always practice safe sex and magic(k).

To John

Chapter One

Maura MacGregor held very still under the steady gazes of the three naked gorgons. They dominated the room and made it impossible to look anywhere else. One of the scaly women was extremely beautiful, and the others, eh… not so much. Forked tongues poked through sharpened teeth. They had snakes for hair and a stare that could turn a human into stone.

If only she were human and not a warlock.

And if only the gorgons were real and not painted on her motel wall because being turned to stone at the moment would be better than being subjected to the rantings of an angry motel guest.

She plastered a smile on her face and turned to the family. They had prepaid for a week in what had been her most expensive suite. The mother gripped her hands tight over the eyes of her children. Considering they were teenage boys, the scene would have been comical if not for the fact she'd promised them the best stay in town during each of the woman's six confirmation calls.

Maura said the only thing she could think of, "Damn vandals."

Damn it, Bruce.

Though, vandals couldn't account for the snakes carved to wind around the headboard and dresser. Luckily, those details didn't draw focus quite like the painting.

Janet Butler backed out of the motel room slowly, stepping onto the outside sidewalk. They were a late check in, and there wasn't anywhere else in town for them to go. The woman herded her teenagers toward the parking lot as she checked up and down the walkway like she feared for their lives.

"Walter," the woman commanded in a shrill voice. "Walter, come on, let's get out of here."

Walter sighed, and the corner of his lip twitched ever so slightly as he glanced at the full-frontal nudes on wall. Maura got the impression that the man didn't get much say in his marriage.

"Walter!"

Walter's shoulders slumped a little, and his head hung forward as he moved out the door.

"Tell her we are expecting a full refund," the wife yelled.

Walter nodded but didn't speak.

"And we're going to leave a bad review online," the woman continued. "Walter? Did you tell her?"

Walter peeked at Maura and then through the door at the naked ladies. "I think she heard you, Janet."

"I have other rooms," Maura offered. "I'd be happy to give ya a deep discount for the inconvenience."

The inconvenience of having to step six feet to the left to another door, she added silently.

Somedays she didn't know why she bothered.

"What did she say? I can't understand a thing that comes out of her mouth." Janet had understood her just fine on each of the demanding phone calls, but suddenly Maura's Scottish accent was an issue?

"She said they have other rooms." Walter didn't try to sell his wife on the idea.

"You expect us to stay in a high crime…?" The flustered woman's words trailed off as she pushed her boys toward the parking lot. "Get in the car, boys. Hurry."

Maura slowly pulled the motel room door closed and gestured her hand at the painting, calling forth her magick to remove it from her wall. Yellow sparks hit the paint and made a strange crackling noise before dissipating. The painting remained.

"Omigod, Waa-lter!"

At the panicked sound, Maura turned in time to see her uncle, Raibeart, streaking across the motel parking lot. The teenagers laughed. One lifted his phone, and Maura gave a tiny wave of her fingers to make him drop it before he could hit record.

"I'm nae Walter. The name's MacGregor, love, Raibeart MacGregor," Raibeart yelled. He gave the shocked woman a jaunty wave as he turned the corner to run along the exterior hall enclosure toward more rooms. Her uncle's late-night runs were getting a little too frequent. And definitely too public.

Damn it, Raibeart.

Walter dutifully got into the car as his wife worked herself into further hysterics. Several doors were open, and other guests watched the show. Frowning, Maura waited for the Butlers to pull out of the motel parking lot before making her way down the long sidewalk toward the front lobby. She smiled at the guests as if there had not just been a frenzied woman screeching at her.

She wasn't too worried about the review. After

some time, she could have her cousin Euann take it down for her. He had a way with computers. Though to be fair to Mrs. Butler, there had been a naked painting on the wall, and she was not given what she'd been promised.

Damn it, Bruce!

Maura peered at the motel sign that read "Hotel Motel" in bright letters to confirm the vacancy light was still showing. It was the stupidest name for a business, but it came with the place when they bought it. Bruce had been fighting her on changing it.

Even though highway traffic broke the serenity as the occasional car zoomed past, the air smelled of the nearby woods. The evening was cool and fresh, perfect for relaxing outside. For all of these small pleasures, she was grateful.

Magick needed to take from nature to work. It didn't manifest out of thin air. Everything in life was a balance, and it was an innate understanding that Maura respected.

She preferred the small-town atmosphere to big cities. Green Vallis, Wisconsin, was as close to nature as the MacGregor family could get without moving into a cave. Lush forest surrounded the town, covering rolling hills and thick underbrush. Woodland creatures were numerous.

Even now, by the motel, surrounded by

concrete walls and parking lot pavement, she felt the power of nature feeding her magick. And it wasn't just nature. Ley lines converged beneath the surface coursing with an ancient mystical power as if centuries of magickal byproduct had been gathering into an invisible river flowing under the town.

The other quick way to fuel magick was sex, but she wasn't having any lately. That was the one drawback of a small town and nosy family. Anyone she even thought about dating became the subject of teasing. Well, and sometimes people she would never think about dating.

When they'd lived near Central Park in Manhattan, her dating life had been much better, making up for nature being scarce.

Maura took a deep breath before going inside the front lobby. A bell jingled on the door to announce her entry.

"Be right with ya," Bruce called from the vicinity of her office.

Though small, the lobby had been recently painted. She checked the walls to make sure no naked supernatural beings had appeared in her absence. The walls were fine, but someone had taken all the brochures for local businesses and turned them upside down on the rack. She glanced around before flicking her hand, magickally flipping them so they faced right side up.

Maura stepped behind the long counter of the check-in desk to issue the Butlers a full deposit refund and stop the automatic email inviting them to rate their stay.

She then went to the office to find her brother had taken up residence in her chair. Bruce read an old thrift store paperback. He was the kind of man who would cherish the torn cover and musty, yellowed paper more than a brand-new book that didn't smell of age and dust. It had something to do with discarded, forgotten, once-loved objects.

"Be right with ya?" Maura asked, eyeing his reclined pose. He'd propped his boots up on her desk. The proof of his disruption had scattered all over the office floor in a mess of papers.

"I figured ya would be." He turned a page.

"Why are there three naked Medusas in the royal suite?" Maura gestured her hand at the papers to pick them up. They floated and stacked themselves before landing on the desk away from Bruce's feet.

"Only one Medusa," Bruce corrected, not looking up from his book. Paint the color of the gorgons' bodies smudged his fingers and stained his clothes. "The others are her sisters, Stheno and Euryale."

"And why are Medusa, Stheno, and Euryale in the royal suite?"

Bruce tried to hide his smirk. "Would ya have me put them in a single? That seems a little rude for ancient beings."

"What was rude is walking the Butler family into that girlie show ya call art."

"Well, why did ya take them to that room?" he asked, as if the problem was obvious. "The décor isn't finished, and there are naked women on the wall."

"I'm going to hex ya," Maura said under her breath, "and I'm going to bury ya deep after I do. Ma will never find the body."

Her brother didn't appear concerned as he lifted a finger, as if beckoning her to wait as he continued to read.

Maura ran through a list of curses she could enact on him. Maybe she'd use a potion in his coffee and turn him into a snake since he seemed to like the creatures so much.

She'd never do it. Maura was the "reliable" sibling.

Bruce and his twin, Rory, might be over a hundred years older than her, but after several centuries of living the age gap mattered less and less, and she often felt like she was the oldest. No one would ever accuse her brothers of being the responsible MacGregors.

That said, no one would accuse any of the males in the extended family of being the responsible MacGregors. She thought of her streaking embarrassment of an uncle spiriting through the parking lot. Yep, and that man was an elder.

How was this family not doomed?

It wasn't easy to hide an extended family of warlocks in the modern age. In the past, before computers and photographs, they could mesmerize a village and disappear—no big deal. Nowadays, affluent Scottish families tended to draw attention in the American countryside. It didn't help that the men wore kilts and walked around as if they starred in their own reality television show. If they overstayed their welcome, people began to notice the family didn't age. There always seemed to be one amateur sleuth who started putting things together—usually wrongly together, but together.

Maura crossed her arms over her chest and tapped her foot in irritation. "Bruce, we need to discuss this."

Bruce lowered his book, marking his page with his finger, and focused a stern stare in her direction. "Would ya please make up your mind? First ya tell me I have to get rid of the cherub suite because no one wants to see naked Cupid butts first thing in the morning. So I fix it, and ya are still complaining."

"I don't want naked anything in the hotel rooms."

"Motel," Bruce corrected. "We're a motel. Doors are on the outside, not inside. Don't try to fancy it up."

"I don't want naked anything in the *motel* rooms."

"Ya do know what guests do in the—"

"Art," Maura interrupted. "I don't want naked art. At least go paint bikinis on the triplets because, for some reason, my magick is not working to remove the paint ya used."

"Uncle Raibeart and I enchanted it," Bruce answered. "He gave me the idea of the gorgons."

"Of course ya did, and of course he did." Maura shook her head.

Bruce turned back to his book. "Well, ya weren't very specific."

"I said I wanted taupe walls." Maura leaned over her desk and flicked the back of his ear. "That's pretty specific."

He jerked his head away from her, pretending it hurt more than it did. "Och, I thought ya were joking, lassie. Taupe? That's not creative. Where's your imagination? Your heart? Taupe is what they use in prison as a punishment to bore ya to death. Taupe is what they put in hospital waiting rooms to make ya feel sedated before they cut off your balls."

She tried to hide her laugh and failed. "What hospitals are ya going to? A vet?"

Bruce tilted his head in thought and drummed his fingers on the desktop. "Ya know, I can't remember. The last time had to be one of the wars, and it was more tent than a hospital."

Maura stared at his tapping fingers. Flashes of violence clouded Maura's thoughts, memories of broken bones, whippings outside a large white house, and crying babies that didn't feel like they belonged inside her head. And blood. So much blood. Rivers of it. She'd lived through much, and had probably forgotten a great portion of it, but these recollections didn't feel like hers. She'd never been on a slave plantation.

"Did I say something?" Bruce's playful expression dropped into one of concern. His fingers stopped their drumming.

"Just…" She shook her head. "Nothing."

"Still having those nightmares?"

"Aye." Maura nodded. "Ma's convinced it's because I fall asleep watching the television. She says the transmission waves scramble my dreams. The truth is silence makes them worse."

"She also thinks video games rot the brain," Bruce chuckled. "I'm living proof that's not true."

"I don't know that I would use that example to argue your point," Maura teased, drawing attention away from her recurring nightmares. It was bad enough she had to live with them at night. She didn't want to talk about them when she was awake too. She'd tried every spell and potion she could find to make them stop. Nothing had worked.

"I'm curious about something." Bruce furrowed his brow in deep thought. "Do nurses still wear those cute white dresses and hats? I do like a lady in uniform. Maybe it's time I checked out a hospital."

"Bruce, I need ya to concentrate." Maura directed her most stern look at him. "Please be serious for once. I need your help. Ya know the family expects us to show a profit in the first year running. We need guests to actually stay here to make that happen. We do not want to be the bottom tier business on the MacGregor spreadsheet."

"Never cared for bookkeeping," Bruce said. "Besides, that distant fifth cousin twice removed of ours always comes in last. How much money does the family really need?"

"Can ya just—*I don't know*—paint all the

rooms in a way to express the banality of modern life?"

"I could…" Bruce inched his way past her toward the door of the small office. "But, Maura, isn't it vain for ya to have your portrait in *every* room?"

Bruce laughed and darted for the door. Maura flung her hand, sending the newly stacked papers to pelt him in the back. He laughed harder.

Maura sat down at her desk and flicked her wrist to call back the papers she'd thrown. Taking over the Hotel Motel had not been her idea. Mini bars and towel counts weren't part of her dream job.

Then again, she really didn't have a dream job.

Or a dream vacation.

Or a dream life.

Or a dream *anything*.

She did have nightmares of blood, but it wasn't the same thing.

So it became that owning a motel was her current endeavor. Everyone in the MacGregor family worked and contributed. Though being a lazy, rich dilettante did have appeal, the truth was without purpose immortality became challenging to live.

Maura often equated a MacGregor family

move into a new town like a swarm of locusts invading. It wasn't just a few of them. It was the entire extended family—all the siblings from her parents' generation and their children. Eventually, some of the extended-extended family would show up. They arrived in a flurry, and before the townspeople knew what was happening, they overtook everything. It sounded harsher than it was in reality. Communities thrived. Animal shelters became well-funded—a pet project of Uncle Raibeart's. MacGregor businesses provided jobs with real benefits. The family also protected locals against the supernatural threats they didn't know existed in the world. Though, to be honest, those supernatural threats normally arrived because the MacGregors lived there.

Maura shivered, and she stood from her desk. The air changed. It developed a peculiar feel, a heaviness like the seconds before the first raindrops, but there had been no clouds in the sky when she'd come inside.

"Bruce, do ya feel…?" Her words trailed off as she realized her brother was no longer in the lobby.

Maura made her way past the check-in desk to gaze outside. Newly formed clouds cast shadows in the moonlight. She pushed through the door so slowly the bell didn't jingle. Her scalp tingled as a static electrical charge filled the air. The subtle change in the surroundings would be unnoticeable to most, but she had lived long enough to know to trust her intuition.

Something was off.

One of the guests played his television a little too loudly, and she heard the rhythmic pattering of battle drums. She saw the set's lights flashing through a window which seemed to indicate the source of the noise. The eerie sound backdropped against the turning weather caused a chill to work over her spine. Mist rolled into the parking lot on a breeze, and she had the strongest urge to run.

Maura fortified herself, facing her fear as she stared at the mist, attempting to see within its murky depths. Tension filled her, and magick prickled the tips of her fingers, readying for a fight. Whatever this was, all was not right in the town of Green Vallis tonight.

Chapter Two

"Curtis Jefferson." The whispery voice cracked as if dust had settled on the vocal cords.

Self-preservation instantly urged Curtis to run. Logic told him he'd never escape. This was the kind of moment he'd dreaded his entire life.

Curtis slowly lowered the bag of trash he carried to the ground. He placed it beside the dumpster behind Crimson Tavern instead of throwing it over the top. This was one dangerous being he did not want to startle into action.

"You're a hard man to track down," Virgile continued.

Curtis doubted that.

He had only heard the vampire's voice a couple of times, but some living nightmares were impossible to forget. Never had the creature spoken to him directly.

Keeping his hands lifted slightly at his sides, Curtis turned toward the vampire. The soft Southern accent reminded him of his mawmaw's home in the Mississippi Delta. The reminiscence brought with it a mix of nostalgia and fear. His dhampir grandmother had raised him in his later teen years after the death of her son, Curtis's father. His mother, a human, had not lived through his birth. Curtis had sucked the life out of her before he even took his first breath. Curtis's father had never forgiven himself for getting her pregnant, and Curtis's presence had reminded the man of that sin.

Curtis was a third generation dhampir. A vampire had seduced—*a word he used sardonically*— a house slave, producing his grandmother from the union. Mawmaw had warned him that his blood made him easy for vampires to track, and he always needed to be on guard. It was a two-way street. His dhampir blood would warn him when vampires were near, but he had to keep focused and alert.

Tonight, he had failed that lesson. If he hadn't been so preoccupied with food inventory, he would have sensed the vampire skulking in the shadows.

A blur sped past him, triggering one of the alleyway's security lights. Cold fingers clamped his shoulders from behind. Fingernails pressed through his shirt to dig at his skin.

"Why didn't you say goodbye to us?" Virgile pouted. "You know it hurts the sire's feelings when you don't show respect."

Virgile enjoyed the drama of being a vampire, like he'd watched too many Hollywood movies and had adjusted his personality accordingly. Curtis had even seen the vampire make claw hands and hiss at someone. If a messy bloodbath hadn't followed the gesture, it would have been mock-worthy.

Curtis swallowed nervously and closed his eyes. He prayed that this moment would pass with no more than fear-inducing scolding.

Virgile tsked in his ear. "Bad little dhampir. You just snuck away in the middle of the day. Not so much as a goodbye letter."

Curtis wasn't sure why that would have been a concern. He'd never been forced to check in with his vampire great grandfather in the past. The creature barely registered that he existed—or so Curtis assumed—and had never shown genuine interest in him before besides the handful of visits to make an accounting of his human bastard family. It always felt more like business inventory than genuine affection. That was the way Curtis preferred it.

"Had to follow the work," Curtis finally answered. Though his voice was calm, he knew the vampire listened to the rapid beat of his heart and could smell even the tiniest hint of fear.

Virgile spun him around. The security light glinted in the vampire's eyes. The man wore dark eyeliner, long hair, and black clothing with a row of shiny silver buckles down the front of his shirt. He kept his hard hold on Curtis's shoulders. "I don't think it was the work that drew you, garbageman."

Curtis gestured toward the back door, which still hung open. "Crimson Tavern. It's a restaurant, a bar and grill. I run it. I'm not hiding."

Curtis sent money back to his grandmother to help cover her expenses. At over one-hundred-and-fifty years old, she didn't need to be working. It's not like great grandpa ever kicked in to help support his daughter, even though the vampire had acquired a fortune off the deaths of his victims. It didn't matter. Mawmaw would not have wanted his blood money.

"Restaurant? Why don't you show me?" Virgile hooked his arm around Curtis's neck. He smiled to show his fangs. "I could eat."

Curtis didn't want to invite Virgile in to dine

—not because of some antiquated Victorian notion that a vampire needed an invite, which was purely myth, but because bringing Virgile inside would kill his business.

Literally.

Thankfully, it was twenty minutes until closing time, and most of the guests had left.

"That's not a good idea," Curtis said. "This is a small town. People will take notice. Perhaps you should try Green Bay? Or Chicago's not far."

Anywhere that isn't here, he thought.

"People will take notice?" Virgile tilted his head. "Or warlocks?"

Curtis didn't answer. He couldn't deny knowledge of the Scottish family that had moved into Green Vallis not long before him. It wasn't like a bunch of rowdy MacGregors running around in kilts blended into the small-town Wisconsin's landscape. Curtis had instantly detected they were more than eccentric humans the second they walked into his restaurant. His natural avoidance of supernatural beings had transferred onto the MacGregor family, and he kept his distance.

"What would your mawmaw say if she knew you were franchising with the enemy?"

Fraternizing. Curtis resisted the urge to correct a temperamental vampire.

"I can't control who lives here," Curtis answered.

"You control that you live here." Virgile's grip tightened.

"Hey, Jennifer, how've you been?" Kay's shout carried from within the restaurant. The woman worked for him and was the only waitress on shift since Jennifer had given her notice. Actually, Jennifer quit because she fell in love with a MacGregor, Rory. If Jennifer was here, then that meant the MacGregors were probably with her.

Panic knotted his insides. His business had just started to turn a profit. Virgile's presence would ruin everything.

The MacGregors knew Curtis wasn't entirely human. They'd sensed it almost immediately. Though, he had lied to the warlocks when he told them he didn't know which vampire sired his line. That connection was the family secret.

Or, more precisely, that connection was the family shame. Who would want to admit to an immortal war criminal in the family genetics? They avoided talk of it whenever possible. It's not like Ole Grandpappy Buford came to the reunions. Of course, those reunions were always in the middle of a Mississippi August day when the sun was hot and bright, but that was beside the point.

Virgile stared at him. The intensity of his gaze was caught somewhere between curiosity and intimidation. Or maybe it was confusion. Immortality didn't automatically come with a higher IQ. Virgile was a lackey, plain and simple.

Curtis tried to think of something to say, but there was no telling what would set Virgile off. For a moment, the vampire's grip on him loosened, and he thought Virgile was going to let him go.

Suddenly, his entire body jerked violently, and the back alley blurred. Curtis tried to hold his breath as the vampire sped him between buildings and into the nearby forest. When they stopped, moonlight barely invaded the thick canopy overhead, but it was enough to see the bat-like features fading from Virgile's face as he shifted back to his human form.

Virgile paced in the darkness, blending into the thick shadows. "Did you really think warlocks could protect you?"

The only thing worse than Virgile's anger was his boredom. Not that it mattered, both were deadly.

"You never learn, do you? You just keep coming back to this moment. To her."

Curtis frowned. "Her?"

"The sire wants to see you. He's tired of the game," Virgile stated. "I'd say to pack a bag, but I don't think you'll need clothes where you're going."

"What her? What game?" Curtis insisted. "I swear I don't know what you're talking about. I came here because the tavern was for sale, cheap, and I always wanted my own restaurant. Are you sure he's looking for me? Maybe you're thinking of someone else."

Curtis had always sworn to himself that if a moment like this came, he would never give them the satisfaction of begging. Maybe that lie had provided comfort at the time but being faced with the reality was another story. Fear took over. Vampires had imaginative ways of killing people. He slowly inched back, wondering how deep into the woods they'd traveled.

If he ran, would he find help?

Then again, who would help him?

"You bore me, you sack of rotted blood."

Shit.

Virgile studied him. "You *would* be lighter to carry without legs."

"You know he won't be happy if you bring him the wrong man." It was a weak argument, and they both knew it. He took another step back and tripped, landing hard on his backside.

"You really don't know a thing, do you?" Virgile laughed, looming over him.

"Why are you doing this? I haven't done any—"

"But you have." Virgile threaded his hands behind his back and leaned down. Tension radiated from his stiff body.

"I was never given an order to stay in Mississippi." Curtis felt around on the ground, trying to crawl back to safety. His hand moved through the forest litter of dead leaves.

"You were not given permission to leave."

"My phone number remained the same. I'm reachable."

Virgile appeared surprised by the defense, which only served to piss the vampire off more. "If it were up to me, I'd have killed your mawmaw the day she was born and been rid of the lot of you half breed—"

Curtis's hand hit a piece of rotted wood, and he reacted on instinct, thrusting the branch up for protection just as Virgile lunged forward with extended hands. The branch lodged between them. It stabbed Curtis in the stomach. His body tensed, and he cried out in pain.

Virgile's expression widened in surprise, and he stumbled back, taking the branch with him. Curtis rolled on the ground and pushed to his feet, intent on running away.

Virgile screamed. Curtis swayed, grabbing his bleeding stomach.

The branch protruded from the vampire's chest. Soot coated his features as he burned from within. Curtis had seen vampire death as a child, and the creatures never went peacefully. His mawmaw said it was all the pain they'd caused in life being revisited upon them tenfold. If that were true, Virgile would be in agony.

The vampire's screams turned into high-pitched screeches. Curtis covered his ears as the reverberation in his head became worse than the pain in his bleeding stomach.

The death fire broke through tiny cracks in Virgile's skin. He reached forward as if to grab onto Curtis, hands clutching into fists. His knee lifted, but the calf did not go with it as the limb split into two. The now-legless vampire plummeted to the ground and exploded into a blaze of ash and fire until all that remained was the charred leg standing in the remains of a cowboy boot.

The canopy of treetops caught fire. Flames instantly ate through branches. The loud crack of breaking limbs echoed before they rained down on the dry bed of dead leaves below. One hit close to the leg causing it to crumble and disappear.

Curtis pressed his hand into his wound, willing

the bleeding to stop. Each step sent a jolt of excruciating awareness through him, and he grunted in pain as he ambled toward safety. With his free hand, he braced against tree trunks and branches to stay upright. With every slow step of progress, he knew the flames were closer to catching up to him.

"What fool lights a bonfire in the middle of a forest?" The Scottish accent automatically gave away the fact she was a MacGregor.

The woman's irritation caused him to halt his progress. He steadied himself against a tree.

A stout wind whipped past him, picking up too quickly to be natural, only to end just as quickly. He took halted steps back toward the fire. The flames swirled into a vortex before extinguishing, and darkness fell over the forest once more.

"I hear ya breathing," the woman said.

The smell of charred wood and burned leaves hung thick in the air. Smoke gathered like fog, rolling over to swallow his legs in the murky depths.

"Show yourself," she commanded.

Curtis shuffled his feet, finding it difficult to walk without being able to see where he stepped. Blood seeped from his wound, coating his fingers.

"I'm warning ya—"

"I mean no harm," Curtis interrupted her threat.

She came out of the shadows into a thin thread of moonlight. Shorter red hair framed her pretty face. Maybe he'd been mistaken. She might not be a MacGregor. She looked a little like a wood nymph. At least, from the stories he'd read, she was pretty enough to be one. Although he didn't remember the nymph in those stories wearing blue jeans and stylish green tops.

"Who are ya?" She studied his face, squinting as if she might have to force an answer from him.

"Curtis Jefferson. I own Crimson Tavern."

"Oh. Right." She relaxed her stance and placed her hand against her chest as she let loose a long breath. "That makes sense. Ya are the dhampir my cousins were telling me about the other day. For a moment, I swore I felt a vampiric presence. The last thing anyone needs is a bunch of human-sized leeches sucking the town dry."

"None taken," Curtis mumbled.

"Sorry?"

"No offense taken," he said, clarifying.

She stepped closer. "I'm sorry. I thought they said ya didn't know the vampire in your family tree. I just assumed..." She stopped herself, lifting her hands to the side. "Forgive me if I inadvertently insulted ya. Let's start over. Hi. I'm Maura

MacGregor. I own Hotel Motel with my brother, Bruce. I do all the work, and he paints obscene pictures on the walls. Yes, I know the name is stupid. It came with the business. We're currently fighting over what to call it."

"Curtis Jefferson. Crimson Tavern." He tried to match her friendly tone, but it became hard to concentrate. "Sounded like a good plan when I made it. No…paint."

He dropped to his knees in the smoke. He expected it to irritate his lungs, but it felt cool like mist.

"Whoa, easy." Maura darted forward to catch him before he collapsed to the side. The movement stirred the mist and a small clearing appeared around them. "Are ya…? Is that blood?"

Her hand pressed over his, applying pressure.

"It's nothing—"

"Shh. Do ya hear that?" Maura glanced around.

Curtis didn't hear anything. He found it difficult to concentrate, so instead stared at her pretty face.

"What's happening here?" she asked.

"I'll be fine." Curtis tried to push her hand away. "I don't know if there are more."

"More what?" Maura wiped her fingers on her leg before taking his face in both hands. "More vampires? Was that a death fire? Are ya out here fighting vampires?"

Curtis's vision dimmed, and he felt himself sliding to the ground. "It's not true. Not all dhampirs are vampire hunters. That's a movie thing. I want nothing to do with them."

"That didn't answer my question." Maura tried to pull him upright, but he had no energy to sit back up.

"You can't be here," Curtis mumbled. "It's not safe for nymphs to be out of the story book."

Chapter Three

Nymphs?

Maura ignored the nonsensical mumblings of the injured man lying on the ground. It's clear he'd lost blood and undoubtedly hit his head. He barely made sense.

Maura ran her fingers through his short, dark brown hair feeling for lumps. His scalp appeared uninjured. She then rubbed the tips of her fingers together, causing them to glow softly with magick. She pried open an eye and used the light to check that the pupil constricted. They were strikingly gorgeous eyes, the dark brown threaded with light.

Maura dropped the eyelid but kept her glowing fingers close to his face. She turned his head to get a better look. The man had been blessed with a good jawline and strong features. They were the perfect showcase to firm lips.

"Where have they been hiding ya?" Maura whispered with a shake of her head.

She had more immediate problems than contemplating her future dating life. Her parents and the other elders wouldn't exactly be thrilled if she brought a dhampir home. They had some antiquated Medieval ways of thinking. Vampire blood being very, very bad was one of them. Of course, some of them remembered the vampiric feeding frenzy that helped spread the bubonic plague.

A light tapping sound caught her attention. Maura extinguished her fingers and listened as the noise grew louder. The drums were back, only there wasn't a television on which to blame the noise this time.

Curtis didn't move. She glanced around, wondering if she could call back the light to see his stomach injury better but thought better of it. The drums became louder, the rhythmic military thrumming punctuated by the march of feet. It was not a sound that belonged in the forests of Wisconsin.

Unsure what else to do, Maura traced her fingertip over Curtis's wound. Tiny yellow lights danced around her finger as she called forth her magick. It petrified the edges, hardening the skin into a stone-like texture to stop the bleeding. She hoped it would work. Typically petrifying spells were meant to turn the whole person into a temporary statue.

The mist stirred around them, causing a chill to work up her spine. The foreboding that had compelled her from the motel parking lot into the woods grew steadily with each ticking second. The phantom music loomed toward them, increasing in intensity.

Ghosts?

Maura tried to hoist Curtis to his feet. He was too heavy for her to carry physically. Magick would only draw attention. Spirits sometimes floated toward magick like mosquitos to a blood buffet.

A figure appeared from inside a tree. The mist parted to give the boy a path.

Her assumption of ghosts had been correct. A drummer boy in a Civil War uniform, no more than thirteen, marched backward as if his time rewound itself. His body was too transparent and the forest too dark to determine what color he wore—blue or gray—but it didn't seem to matter considering there shouldn't be an army in this part of the country—ghosts or not.

The mist moved, creating soldiers to march in

time with the drummer boy. Some were missing arms, and others were headless as if there was not enough mist to finish their forms. The ghosts moved in reverse, passing through the trees as if they weren't there. Maura huddled close to Curtis as the soldiers surrounded them. So far, none of the spirits appeared to sense the living. With luck, it would be a residual haunting, ghost energy trapped in a long-ago moment, completely unaware of their surroundings or that they were lost.

"Curtis?" Maura mouthed more than whispered his name. She lightly tapped his cheek. He didn't respond.

The drummer boy backed toward them. His ghostly steps kept time with the others. Each rap of the drum struck like a warning.

Maura leaned close to Curtis's ear. "We need to get out of here. Curtis, can ya hear me? I need ya to run."

When she again looked up, it appeared as if some of the soldiers had turned their attention toward them. Their heads now faced the wrong direction on their backward marching bodies. The drummer boy was almost upon them. The feeling of dread grew.

Maura wasn't sure what to do, so she shielded Curtis with her body and held her breath as the ghost child marched through them. She pressed against Curtis's prone form and closed her eyes tight. Cold feet pierced into her back like ice-covered knives. Her breath caught, and all she could manage was a grunt of pain. The spirit pulled energy from her, draining her of the ability to move.

The drummer boy marched on, backward steps thumping a little louder than before.

Maura gasped noisily for air, trying to force oxygen into her freezing lungs. The sound of drums faded, taking the marching soldiers with it. The light had improved, and she was able to see the details of his face better. He was definitely cuter than she'd been led to believe by her cousins. The way they'd described it, the dhampir was some sort of deformed knobby creature, an over-grown gremian.

Several long seconds passed before she could find the energy to lift herself away from Curtis's chest. He wore a black button-down shirt with a hole torn in the stomach and dark denim jeans. She lightly pressed her hand to his wound to see if it still bled. Satisfied her petrifying spell was hold-ing, she pushed back on her legs to kneel on the ground to get her bearings.

Maura stiffened in surprise. The ghosts had disappeared, but so had the trees.

Moonlight shone over open prairie. Uncut grasses swayed in a light breeze. A row of trees shadowed the distant landscape. Nothing about the environment felt right—the look, the weather, the smell, the energy her magick summoned from the nearby forest to refuel her ghost-drained powers.

Humidity clung to the air, sticking her shirt to her arms and chest as she stood. She used the bottom hem to fan herself.

"Reveal yourself," she whispered the simple spell.

The magick marked Curtis's body with several blue embers floating up toward the heavens. They dissipated in the breeze. Sparkly blue lights drifted up from the nearby trees, indicating the small forest animals that lived within. A more significant light to her right could have been a mammal, or perhaps a single person. Slower to appear was an intense gathering of lights to her left, high above the trees and miles away to show what might be a distant town or campsite. The number of blue lights denoted there were nearly a hundred people gathered, give or take.

"Doesn't look like anyone will be sneaking up on us, Curtis." Maura wished the man would wake up and help her figure out what was happening. "But it also means no one is coming to help us, and ya need a healer."

Maura tried not to let nervousness control her thinking. Panic didn't help anyone. She thought about sending up a magickal flare. If her family were nearby, they'd come running. If they weren't, she could attract some very negative attention.

Maura again dropped to the ground next to Curtis. She lifted his shirt to reveal his muscular stomach. Dried blood surrounded the petrified puncture wound. She pressed her fingers around the opening, keeping her inspection clinical. The spell she'd used to stop the leak was akin to squirting superglue into an open wound. No healer or doctor would approve. There was no way to determine what internal organs, if any, had been injured.

The spell wouldn't last forever. Soon the wound would start seeping again. They needed to find real help.

Maura unbuttoned his shirt. "Sorry, pal, it's either yours or mine, and I am not running around mystic prairie in my bra."

Undressing an unconscious man wasn't an easy task under normal circumstances, but thankfully her magick made pulling the material off him as effortless as plucking a spiderweb from the air. It slithered from his body like ethereal liquid only to resolidify in her hands.

"Someone's been hitting the gym," Maura observed the definition of Curtis's chest and arms. She might be hundreds of years old, but she wasn't dead inside. "Don't worry. I'm not a pervert. I won't be doing strange stuff to ya in your sleep."

Curtis felt familiar, though she knew she'd never met him. *That* she would have remembered. Maura tried to remember exactly the last time she'd been on a date. It had been long before she came to Green Vallis. The motel took up all of her time, but that was more excuse than anything else.

Why was she thinking about this now?

"Ya are distracting me," Maura scolded. "I need to keep my head on task."

She made quick work of tying the sleeves around his waist to apply pressure to the wound.

"Now, I don't want to worry ya, but I am not sure where we are or how we got here." Maura examined her makeshift bandage. "I'm going to venture a guess and say that wasn't a Civil War reenactment gone awry, which means we could be in some serious supernatural trouble. So, if ya would like to wake up and give insight into our situation, that would be much appreciated."

Curtis didn't move.

"Or ya know, keep sleeping," she muttered sarcastically. "That's helpful too."

Maura stood and slowly turned in a circle as if staring into the shadows would reveal some kind of hidden truth. All she saw was a field at night. They could have been anywhere.

Maura tried not to freak out as she sought the most reasonable explanation. The MacGregors were always pulling pranks on each other. Maybe Bruce thought this would be funny payback for her making him paint over his gorgon porn. Her brother was talented. She just wished he'd pick a different canvas.

Was it possible he'd trapped them in a painting? If Uncle Raibeart helped enchant the paint, there was no telling what would go wrong.

Or could it simply be another nightmare? Her dreams were vivid. Maura rubbed her arms. Though, usually not this vivid, and her nightmares included significantly more blood than one puncture wound.

Hallucinogens? When was the last time she ate? Magick mushrooms were easy enough to find.

But what if her family had nothing to do with this? What if it was a supernatural attack?

"Ow, fuck."

Maura quickly turned to Curtis and fell to her

knees next to him. "I have never been so happy to hear anything in my life."

Curtis tried to sit up. His brow furrowed. "Ow, fuck?"

Maura smiled in relief to see him awake. She nodded.

"Ok, then," he whispered. "Ow, fuck."

"Careful." She guided his arm. "You're pretty badly hurt."

Curtis surveyed their surroundings and frowned. "Where are we? How did we get out of the forest?"

"I don't know," she answered.

"How did we get here?"

"I don't know."

"Where is here?"

"No clue."

"How long was I out?"

"Don't know. Time got a little wobbly. For a while though—"

Curtis slapped his arm. "Dammit!"

Maura jolted in surprise.

"Something bit me," Curtis explained.

Maura leaned to check where he rubbed his shoulder. The sight of his chest in the moonlight held her attention longer than it should have. Thoughts tried to surface. Her imagination was running wild.

What the hell was wrong with her? She kept losing her focus.

Curtis held his stomach and pushed to his feet. "Do you have any clue which way we should go?"

Maura pried her eyes away from him.

"There seems to be a small gathering or something in that direction," Maura pointed toward the distant trees. "I'd guess roughly two or three miles."

"I thought you didn't know where we are. Did you hear them?"

"Ya know what it means that I'm a MacGregor, right?" Maura's family had a rule about outsiders learning about the existence of magick, but Curtis was supernatural, well, half-supernatural. "My cousins told me that ya know about magick, about us and what we do."

"Yeah." He nodded. "I do. When I was growing up, I heard stories about your family from when y'all lived in the South—all good, by the way."

"Like what?"

"That you saved thousands of lives," Curtis said. "They say MacGregor magick can be trusted but to be careful because you have a Loki hiding in your ranks. There is even a painting of one of your ancestors in the local library back home."

"Loki? Ya think one of us is a trickster demon?"

Curtis nodded. "They say he pulls pranks and likes to run around naked."

"Right." Maura should have known.

"Could be you for all I know," he teased.

"Could be. So ya better be careful." She arched a brow and realized she was flirting with him.

Seriously. What the hell was wrong with her.

Focus, Maura.

"My point is, if ya know I'm a MacGregor, then ya know that magick is how I detect people are in that direction. Maybe we'll get lucky, and it'll be Green Vallis." Maura doubted it. Green Vallis would've had more life forces than what she'd witnessed.

"I knew this place was special with those ley lines and whatnot but didn't think they could move people around." Curtis again peered over the field as if it could give him answers. "I think they're maybe part of what drew me here. It felt like signs pointing in this direction, you know."

"My cousin Erik is why we're here. It was his turn to find a place for us to relocate. The second he stepped into town, he'd felt that power. He even bought the giant mansion on the hill that overlooks town—"

"I'm familiar with it," Curtis inserted.

"—without checking with the rest of us first." Maura leaned down and pressed her hands against the warm earth. The grass was soft against her fingers. "I feel nature, enough to easily fuel my magick, but I don't feel the ley lines. I don't think we're close to home."

"Fuel?"

Maura hesitated. Not because she couldn't trust him, but because centuries of being told to keep the MacGregor secrets had been hammered into her head.

"Magick needs to come from somewhere. It doesn't just manifest out of thin air. We warlocks take from nature, converting the energy. It's better if we take a little from a large section rather than a lot from a small one. My family could kill every tree in a tristate area in one go if we wanted." She gave a half smile. "Sex works too for a quick power fix."

Enough with the flirting, Maura, she scolded herself.

"Are you asking if I'll…?" He slowly smiled and looked at the ground. "Here?"

"Easy, lover boy." Maura grinned. "The night is young, and the date just started. I haven't decided if I'm going to let ya kiss me goodbye at the end of the night."

"Well, for the record, if you need to refuel, my services are available." He tightened the sleeves around his waist, grimacing at the applied pressure. "Any chance all this nature fuel means you can magick us back to Crimson Tavern? Kay wasn't planning on locking up after her shift. I just disappeared on her."

"Sorry, all out of magick carpet rides. Though, I wouldn't worry too much. Sheriff Johnson makes regular rounds, and we're not exactly a high-crime area. I'm sure your place will be fine." Maura focused her attention away from him as she considered the route leading to the gathering. "So, coin toss. Do we head toward the people or run from them? I have no clue if they're friend or foe."

"I vote cautiously toward them. Civilization feels safer than the wilderness. We'll find a phone and call for a ride," Curtis said.

"Agree. Besides, ya need a doctor." Maura ducked under his arm and slipped her hand around his waist to support his weight.

"It hurts like a bitch, but I'll be fine." Curtis placed his arm over her shoulder. The breeze helped ease the humidity, but the heat from his body radiated along her side.

"Is that a dhampir thing?" Maura supported

him as they began their journey across the open prairie.

"Yes. Fast healing is one of the only useful things my great grandfather gave me." A small, humorless laugh followed the statement.

"I meant the tough guy act," Maura teased. If not for the fact they were magickally lost, he was injured, and they had just met, this might have been considered a nice night for a romantic stroll.

He nodded. "Yeah, probably that too."

Her mind kept trying to wander away from the reality of the danger they were facing. There was a comfort to the energy between them, a familiarity like she'd known him a long time.

"What else did he give ya, your great grandfather? Ya said that was one of the things." She wanted to keep him talking, hopefully taking his mind off any pain.

Curtis laughed. "The need to pack extra sunblock. The other kids at school used to tease me because I sunburned so badly. They started calling me Crispy."

"Ah, that's kind of cute. Crispy Curtis."

"Don't even." He lifted a finger in warning but smiled to soften the benign threat. "It took me years to outgrow that horrible nickname."

"Before ya fainted, ya said something about not

knowing if there were more." Maura kept an eye on the empty field. "It was a vampire, wasn't it? That is how the fire started. Ya killed it, and those were the death flames. Is there a den near Green Vallis?"

He took several steps before answering. "I need you to know it was an accident. I didn't mean to kill him. I don't want to bring trouble."

"No one is going to be mad that one less vampire is in the world."

"Except maybe other vampires." Curtis took a deep breath, the sound a little ragged, and she wondered if he was in a lot of pain. "I was minding my own business. Virgile abducted me from the alley behind the tavern when I went to take the trash out. After he brought me to the woods, he attacked, and I lifted a piece of wood to block him. I'm not sure if I stabbed him or he landed on the branch and stabbed both of us."

"Sounds like a clear-cut case of self-defense to me.

He inhaled deeply. "Hey, do you smell that?"

"Nothing out of the ordinary." Maura didn't smell anything but nature tinged with sweat. "What about the ghost army that came after?"

"Ghost army?" Curtis started to laugh but stopped. He glanced around without letting go of her. "Wait, seriously?"

Maura nodded. "Civil War troops, drummer

boy, all of it. Have ya ever seen anything like that? They marched over us, and we were transported here."

Curtis dropped his arm from around her shoulders and walked in a small circle to study the landscape. "I would almost bet that a magnolia tree was nearby. They grow all along my mawmaw's property."

Maura took a deep breath. She smelled grass with a hint of flowers, but nothing to cause her notice or alarm.

"I'd know that scent anywhere. Magnolia trees on a Mississippi night." He inhaled and made a slight noise of appreciation. "Come to think of it. They used to tell stories of a ghost army around the campfire when we were kids. I never believed them. The South is full of ghosts, and stories, and superstitions. Mawmaw kept a bottle tree in the front yard to capture ghosts. On hot summer nights, about all you could do is sit in the breeze spinning yarns."

"Spinning...? Oh, aye, telling stories. Right." Maura watched him move without her assistance. Moonlight shifted the shadows over his muscular chest as he lifted his arms over his head to stretch. "Ya don't move like ya needed my support."

"I told you I'd be fine." Curtis grinned, a completely endearing look. "But it's not like I'm going to turn down the opportunity when a pretty woman wraps her arms around me. Mawmaw didn't raise no fool."

Maura laughed. "Easy Casanova. Let's try to stay on subject. We both seem to have the gift of straying off-topic. How did the ghost army stories go?"

"There are variations. Most agree that the ghosts march backward in an attempt to rewind time away from their deaths on the battlefield. Some people considered it an omen—change your ways, or you'll spend eternity running from your sins, or some such nonsense. Others say if they march past you, they'll pull you back in time to suffer with them."

At that, he frowned and lowered his arms to his sides.

"Time travel?" Maura felt sick to her stomach as a new worry took root. "That takes some fucked up, seriously dangerous magick. Warlocks won't mess with that kind of trouble. There are too many variables. Ya change the past, ya change the future. Ya die in the past, ya could have never lived in the future—depending on the spell and whether or not ya went back to inhabit your old body or came back as a second body. And all that is if ya can even pull the spell off."

Maura rubbed her arms, wishing someone

from her family would just appear and help them. She'd even take drunk Uncle Raibeart sprinting across the field.

"No. No. Time travel isn't easy, and those recipes are guarded by the elders with more boobytraps than an '80s movie." She shook her head. "We'd be more likely to stumble into a fairy ring."

"Kind of feels like you're protesting the idea a little too much," Curtis observed.

"I'll admit, I don't want it to be true, but I think sideway travel is more likely than backward travel." She motioned for him to resume walking with her as they made their way toward where her magick indicated people. "Let's find out who's here with us. I don't think a smell and moonlit prairie are going to reveal the answers."

After centuries of living, the unknown normally didn't scare Maura. If anything, she knew that there was no point in working herself up until she had facts. However, currently, that wasn't holding true. The sense of foreboding she'd felt outside the motel tried to return.

Maura told herself that there was no foreseeable danger coming at them, no dire choice to be made or worry over. All they could do was walk, so that is what they needed to do. Walk.

"Your great grandad was the family vampire,

then?" Maura prompted after they'd gone in silence for several minutes. They were still several yards from the woods.

"He is. Mawmaw Abigail's father." Curtis nodded. "It's not something anyone in the family speaks of with pride."

"Have ya met him?"

Curtis didn't answer.

"Curtis?"

He sighed. "I've spent a lifetime not talking about him, even denying knowing him."

"Is that the vampire ya…that died tonight?"

He shook his head. "No."

Maura gently touched his arm. The energy that continually followed between them became more substantial when they made contact. She felt herself gravitating closer to him. "I promise, I'm not judging ya. We can't help the circumstance of our birth."

"I've met my great grandfather a handful of times and would be happy never to meet him again. He visited my father a couple of times before he died and didn't seem to have much interest in me. I didn't realize it until tonight, but apparently, he does keep tabs on what I do. He wasn't happy that I moved to Wisconsin."

Maura sensed that he was maybe holding back. "Who is it?"

"His name's Buford."

She didn't recognize the name.

"He owned a plantation back in the Antebellum South and ate his way up and down the Delta," he continued. "Slavery and the atrocities of war were his nirvana. To hear my mawmaw tell it, a vampire seduced a house slave, and so our genetic line of the family tree was born. I think she comes from an era where Southerners sugarcoated things a little too much. From what I have pieced together, the truth is Buford tortured and raped my great grandmother. There was no seduction about it. She died giving birth to my mawmaw. Human women pregnant with a dhampir child never come to a good end. That's how my mother died, giving birth to me. My mawmaw faired all right because she was also a dhampir. I decided a long time ago that this family line is going to end with me. I'm not putting this curse on another child, and I'm not killing a woman to do it."

Maura didn't try to comfort him. What could she say? It was an awful story. "Then who was in the woods tonight?"

"Virgile. One of Buford's lackeys. Like I was saying earlier, I just found out I'm in a little bit of trouble with my great grandpa. I didn't get his permission before moving out of state and living my life."

"I—" Before Maura could finish the thought, the sound of horse hooves thundered in the distance.

Curtis threw his arm around her and dragged her to the ground. Maura's chest pressed down into the tall grasses—not exactly in the most comfortable of positions. He leaned over her to act as a human shield while he watched for the intruder.

"This is chivalrous and all, but I can handle myself," Maura whispered.

Curtis slowly moved from shielding her and tugged at her arm. When she looked at him, he nodded his head in the direction of his stare.

Maura slowly pushed up from the tall grass to see a man wearing a slouch hat and a Confederate jacket riding a horse. He traveled with purpose, not paying attention to the landscape as he focused his full attention on the path ahead.

Curtis didn't move.

"Please tell me that's a reenactor," Maura said softly.

At her voice, the rider's attention turned toward them, and the horse reacted. His eyes glimmered with an unnatural light. The animal kicked its back legs a little higher.

"Hey!" the rider yelled. His arm moved as if reaching for a gun.

Maura hesitated before she pointed at the man. A blast of magick shot from her hand to strike him from the horse. The man cried out in surprise before landing on the ground.

"What did you do?" Curtis scrambled to his feet.

Maura shot up and ran to see who she'd attacked. Curtis joined her, pushing ahead of her to block her with his shoulder.

"We're in no danger." Maura patted his arm as she sidestepped him. She kicked the rider lightly on the leg. "He'll be fine. My magick padded his landing. He'll wake up by morning thinking he's hungover."

"What is he?" Curtis leaned down to examine the man's face.

Maura tapped his hat with her foot to get a better look. Green-tinted skin and deep pockmarks gave a hint to the identity. "Some kind of troll hybrid, maybe."

Maura whistled and waved her hand to call back the horse magickally. "Come on. We'll make better time with a ride."

"What if someone saw you do that?"

"Calculated risk." Maura greeted the horse, stroking its face gently. "There's a good boy."

"Are you sure about this?" Curtis hung back from the animal.

"Ya wanted a magick transport. This is the best I can do." Maura continued to pet the horse. "Do ya ride?"

"I did." Curtis still didn't approach as he eyed the beast warily. "Once. It wasn't pretty. Horses sense my vampire blood and act squirrelly."

"My magick will keep him calm. Ya will be safe with me. I promise." Maura moved to the stirrup and hoisted herself into the saddle. She ran her hand over the horse's neck, letting her magick relax him. She then reached down to Curtis. "All ya have to do is hold on."

Chapter Four

Injured or not, a man would have to be half dead not to notice a woman like Maura bouncing up and down in front of him as the horse trotted along a forest path. Curtis tried not to focus on the teasing brush of her body against his, or the smell of her hair, or the sound of her voice when she gave her soft commands. She was a hard woman to ignore, especially with their bodies crammed together in the same saddle. Thankfully the troll man had an ample backside which made for a roomier than a normal-sized saddle.

Since coming to Green Vallis, Curtis had been trying to keep his head down. All he wanted was to make enough money to live comfortably and take care of his mawmaw in her golden years.

She'd given so much for him. He wanted to provide for her. Wisconsin was supposed to be a new start.

Maura sat in front of him, steering the animal. Whatever magick she used to keep the horse calm worked. He hadn't been joking when he said the other time that he'd ridden hadn't gone well. The horse had bucked him off and caused a stampede. The local fair had requested he not come back.

Curtis closed his eyes, feeling each place their bodies touched. His hand flexed as he thought about running his fingers through her hair and over her skin. He'd been so focused on work that he'd completely neglected his love life, and his erection chose now to remind him of it.

"Curtis?" Maura asked. "Did ya hear me?"

"Uh, no, sorry, what did you say?" He took a deep breath. It was a mistake. The scent of her hair filled him.

"Can ya check the saddlebags for clues, please?" Maura nudged the horse with her knee as it turned down a slight incline in the path. Trees flanked both sides, and the darkness made it impossible to see between them.

Curtis turned awkwardly in his seat to reach the bags hanging behind the saddle. He dug into one pocket and pulled out something covered in cloth.

"What'd ya find?" she asked.

Curtis unwrapped the material to find a torn loaf of hard bread and dried meat. "Dinner." He sniffed the jerky. "Smells all right. Is troll food edible?"

"Let's find out." She reached over her shoulder and wiggled her fingers.

Curtis handed her a piece of jerky and then took one for himself. He shoved the bread back into the bag and came back out with a brown liquor bottle. He reached it around her and shook the liquor. "Got dessert here, too."

"Mm, now you're talking," Maura said around a mouthful of jerky. "Find anything else?"

She pulled the cork on the bottle and sniffed it.

"Still looking." Curtis checked the saddlebag on the other side. His fingers brushed against a stack of papers, and he began pulling the items out. "Letters. They have wax seals." He set them between them so they wouldn't fall and then reached back into the bag. "Knife. Pistol. Black powder single shot if I'm not mistaken."

"I'm not sure we should drink the troll wine." She handed the bottle back. "Smells off."

Curtis gave Maura the letters and took the bottle for himself. He pulled the cork and sniffed, detecting a metallic scent. Frowning, he poured a little on the back of his wrist. Dark, thick liquid ran over his hand and down his fingers. The unmistakable tingle against his flesh filled him with awareness. Only one thing caused that kind of burning reaction. The horse tossed his head back in protest, and Maura quickly got the animal under control.

"I think it's blood." Curtis shoved the bottle back into the bag. He flicked his hand to get rid of the sensation.

Maura rubbed the tips of her fingers, causing them to glow. She held up the bundle of letters and used her fingers for light. Angling them so he could see, she said, "They are addressed to Sir Buford."

Curtis frowned, correcting, "Sire Buford."

She glanced at them again and nodded. "Aye. Sire."

Curtis sighed. It was possible this reenactment of times gone by was done to satisfy the sadistic whim of a vampire. The modern age must have appeared boring to the satanic monster. At least he hoped that was all this was.

"I'm not sure we should keep going this direction," Curtis said. "If this is a delivery for Buford, we're heading straight for him."

"Aye, I think ya might be—"

"Hold!" A dark shadow of a man suddenly stepped in front of them on the worn path.

Maura quickly extinguished her glowing fingers. The horse neighed and instantly came to a stop before pawing at the ground.

"What was that?" the man demanded, angling his rifle in warning. The country accent reminded Curtis of home.

Curtis detected the shape of the man's hat and the style of his shirt. The rifleman didn't appear to be anything more than human. It would seem the role-playing continued.

"Moonlight?" Maura responded.

"Keep quiet, sweetheart. No one's talking to you." The man spat on the ground.

Curtis grimaced and tensed. He lifted his hand as he began to rebuff the man's dismissing tone when Maura touched his leg and squeezed lightly. In that slight caress, he felt her telling him to be calm just as she had the horse.

"You're late." The man came to stand near their legs. The dim light did not reveal much of the rifleman's face, and Curtis had to assume the man couldn't make out his features either. "Where's the troll?"

"He got held up," Curtis said.

A man shouted in the distance. The tone sounded more like a command than anything else, though he couldn't make out the exact words.

The guard grumbled to himself. "Do you have the delivery? The master's waiting."

"Uh, yeah, sure…" Curtis reached into the saddlebag and handed the bottle down to the man. "We were told to give him this."

Maura started to laugh but covered her mouth with her hand and coughed instead.

"This it? No letter?" The man took the bottle. "He's not going to be happy about that."

"The troll is coming behind us," Maura answered.

The man grunted when Maura spoke. He put his thumb over the cork and shook the bottle several times. A second shout came from the distance, followed by a loud crack and a high-pitched scream.

"What's going on?" Maura asked.

"Nothing to concern yourself over. You're not to the sire's taste." The man pointed his rifle into the trees. "No horses allowed at the Big House. Stable it near the cabins."

"Where's that?" Curtis asked.

"Half mile that direction. Ask for Old Joe. Rest your horse, and then be on your way in the morning. Trust me. You don't want to be running around these parts at night. Never know what's going to jump up and bite you." The man gave a small charge at them and cackled when they flinched in surprise.

The man aimed his rifle at the sky and fired. The horse bucked back. Curtis wrapped his arm protectively around Maura's waist as she steadied the startled animal. The gunman cackled again as his crunching footsteps retreated into the dark woods from where he'd appeared.

"I'm starting to suspect my uncle Raibeart spiked my drink, and this is all some kind of mind game hallucination," Maura said. "Did ya see that man's costume? And the body odor was unnecessarily authentic."

"Then he would've had to spike both of our drinks because I see it all too," Curtis reasoned.

"If this is some kind of elaborate prank— which I don't think is the case because I can't see my family going to such lengths to mess with me —we have to play it out. If this is some kind of magick spell or curse and we're really in the past, then we still need to play the game to find a way to break it. There's a reason we were brought here."

Curtis placed a hand on her arm. They were astride the horse, bodies pressed close, and he still wanted to draw her closer to him. "If this is Buford playing one of his sadistic games to torture me, I'm sorry you were dragged into it. You were at the wrong place at the wrong time."

"A feeling I couldn't ignore lured me to the forest. I was where I was meant to be." Maura put her hand over his. "I can't explain why, but I feel like I'm supposed to be here with ya. That's the only part of this whole night that makes sense."

"This is one hell of a supernatural blind date —ghost armies, time travel, grand theft horse, bad jerky, and bottles of blood." Curtis chuckled. "Call me old-fashioned, but I would have preferred cooking ya dinner and maybe a movie."

"Sadly, this isn't the worst date I've ever been on, and that's saying a lot. It beats the time my cousin Malina convinced me to go on a double with her. She set me up with a werewolf."

"Oh, yeah? Don't like hairy men?"

"It was a full moon. He tried to eat me, and I had to turn him into a statue." Maura dropped her hand from his and nudged the horse. It began to move as if it knew the way to go. She ducked under a low branch prompting him to do the same. "That would have been fine, but the statue was in the middle of the town square. The next morning tourists noticed. We were in Italy at the time. People were taking pictures. I had to stay out there all day and make sure he didn't start to thaw in front of everyone. The next night we got him out of there. Suddenly, his picture is in the paper, and people are talking about how a beloved town sculpture was stolen. To make matters worse, Malina confessed the whole—*what she deemed hilarious*—story to the family. It turns out this guy is some kind of magickal heir to a werewolf fortune. My ma and his ma start making plans like we're going to have a royal wedding."

They leaned to the side to miss another branch.

"Obviously, it ended well, right?" He wished he could see her face while she spoke. "I mean, you're not married, are you?"

Oh, he hoped not.

Maura gave a small laugh. "Not that I recall."

There was a God.

The sound of the distant screams became louder, cutting off the conversational digression. They both turned in the direction of the noise as if they could somehow detect what happened through the trees.

"We should help that woman." Maura nudged the horse so it would go faster.

Curtis felt the same, but he also needed to protect Maura. If Buford was close, they didn't want to draw his attention. The vampire would be all too eager to have a beautiful MacGregor warlock under his control. What man wouldn't?

"I don't sense anyone else around us," Maura said, more to herself. She rubbed her fingertips to bring back the glow. She snapped the wax seal on one of the letters. "Might as well take a peek. It's not like we're going to pony express these to Buford."

"What does it say?" Curtis tried to lift in his seat to read over her shoulder.

Maura used her fingertips to trace across the lines. "Bill of sale." She opened a second one. "Also a bill of sale."

"For what?"

"People." Maura frowned. "It's dated June 1864."

"That's in the middle of the Civil War," Curtis answered.

Maura broke open the next one. "This looks like…"

"What?"

"Some kind of prophecy. It's recommending that he kill—" A scream pierced the night, more agonized than before. Maura jolted in her seat. The horse responded to her movement and whinnied. When she managed to calm the animal, she said, "It recommends killing the child before it's born. Otherwise, he'll have to wait and fight… something… the ink is a little smudged."

"Kill a baby?" Curtis took a deep breath and

his fists clenched. "I am not a murderous man, but he is one creature I wouldn't hesitate to put down. The stories I've heard whispered about him, the things that he has done…"

"I wouldn't stop ya," Maura admitted.

Curtis released his fists and pressed the flat of his hands to his thighs. "Too bad he's so powerful. We'd probably never get close enough to try."

"I recognize this seal. It's from an order of wizards who practiced dark magick. They follow the suffering of humans and would have been active in the United States during the 1800s." Maura held the letter closer to her face. "Looks like they made this prediction at Buford's request. Oh, no."

"What?"

"It didn't say to kill *the* child. It says to kill *his* child." Maura clutched the paper in her hand. "It's talking about your grandmother. I think I know why fate or whoever sent us here. We are meant to intercede and save her. June 1864, does that mean anything to ya?"

"I…" Curtis shook his head. "I don't think so."

"When was your grandmother born?"

"Mawmaw never liked to talk about it. When she was little, they didn't exactly keep birth records, but it could have been around this time."

Curtis snatched the letter from her, trying to read it in the dark. "She kept changing the date to lie about her real age. Some of it might have been vanity, but mostly it was to explain why she wasn't aging like other people. But, yeah, she would have been born into slavery, so it's possible."

Lanternlight illuminated the darkness. Curtis shoved the letters into his pocket to hide them. Maura extinguished her fingers.

"Follow me." The sound of the man's voice was weathered by age and weariness. The lantern began to move. "We were expectin' you earlier, but the food's still warm if y'all are hungry."

Maura swung down off the horse, and Curtis gratefully joined her on the ground. He stretched his legs, only now realizing how sore they were from the saddle.

"Take the horse," the man ordered a nearby boy who instantly did as he was told.

A couple of dozen raised cabins were placed closely together in two rows to create an almost-town with one dirt road running through the middle. No one was outside beside the older adult and the kid. The unpainted wood siding had lost its fight against the sun and had started to warp. Small, covered porches were held in place with wooden beams, a few of which had broken into two and caused the adjoining roof to sag. Doors and windows were shut with bundles of weeds hanging from them like talismans. With the heat and humidity, it had to be boiling inside the homes.

The screams became louder as they came out of trees into a clearing.

"Who is that?" Maura asked.

"Sorry, ma'am?" The man turned, holding up the lantern to look more thoroughly at them. He frowned, eyeing first Maura and then Curtis. His gaze moved over their clothing. "I'll have Ida take you to one of the neighbors. It's a long ride, but you shouldn't be out here, ma'am. This is no place for a lady."

"I'll be fine here," Maura assured him.

The old man stared at Curtis as if imploring him to help convince her. Having been raised in the South on stories of the past, Curtis knew all of the fears this man felt and why. "She'll be fine."

"Are you one of..." The old man glanced between the two visitors and thought better of asking his question. "Are you hungry? Ida will heat some supper."

"That's awfully kind of you, sir." Curtis held out his hand. "I'm Curtis. This is Maura."

"Folks call me Old Joe," the man answered, not taking Curtis's offered hand but instead giving a small wave, "on account there are sixteen Joes here, and I'm the oldest."

The screaming continued. Warning bells went off in his head. Curtis shared a look with Maura.

She leaned close and whispered, "Vampires are near."

Curtis nodded. He'd felt them too.

"Ida!" Old Joe yelled.

"She went to help Miss Hazel birth her baby." The boy who'd taken the horse reappeared from around the side of a nearby cabin.

"Get inside. Lock in before they take you from your bed," Old Joe ordered. The boy was slow to obey as he stared at Maura, but he eventually went into the home.

"Miss Hazel?" Curtis prompted. "Is that—?" He lifted his hand as another scream pierced the night.

Old Joe nodded. "Poor girl. This is the most anyone has heard her voice since it happened."

Maura touched Curtis's arm. He nodded at her meaningful look.

"We need you to take us to Hazel," Curtis said.

Old Joe shook his head in denial. "This is no place for wanderin'. You're best off inside. We don't have much, but your welcome to share it."

"I was sent to help. I'm a midwife." Maura

lifted her hand toward Joe and took slow steps toward him. Tiny lights appeared around her fingers as she touched the man's arm. "Ya want to take us there."

Old Joe slowly nodded. "Sure thing. This way."

Chapter Five

"There." Old Joe pointed at a cabin set aside from the others before quickly retreating.

"Thank—" Maura barely got the word out before he was too far away to hear it, and she wasn't about to start yelling in the middle of the night with vampires in the area. Sure, they could already probably detect her, but there was no point in drawing attention.

Curtis stayed close to her side. She felt his nervous energy as if it were her own and couldn't blame him for it. They were about to walk in on the birth of his grandmother.

"You're a midwife?" Curtis asked. "Much call for that in the motel business?"

Maura shook her head. "No. That was a bald-faced lie. I have been present for two births. Both times I assisted my ma, and neither had been by lanternlight with the threat of vampiric danger lingering in the background."

Curtis turned in little circles as they walked, keeping an eye on their surroundings. "Please tell me we're here to help all of these people."

Maura didn't have an answer. Tonight was a night of feeling things she hadn't in a very long time. Right now, that was nervousness. This situation wasn't like any she'd ever experienced before. She wished she had her family with her to back her up if things went sideways. "I'd offer for ya to stay outside while I do this, but I don't think we should separate."

"You know what this means, right," Curtis said. "We're officially in the past. This isn't a game."

More screams came from the cabin.

"That is another problem for another hour." Maura strode toward the screams of the woman in labor. "Luckily, my family exists in this time. In fact, I exist in this time, and I don't remember having met myself. So, we probably didn't do that, or maybe we do. This is why time travel isn't pursued. It messes with the timelines. Alternate realities and all those headache-inducing theories."

The screams became softer.

"As you said, that's a problem for another hour." Curtis rushed ahead of her toward the cabin.

The sun-weathered structure had wood rot along the edges. A dirty cloth hung out of the corner, shoved from inside to plug a hole. She couldn't see any windows to peek inside. Light came along the bottom edge of the door. A small porch was made out of misshapen boards resting on the ground. They creaked as they stepped onto them.

"Hush her up!" someone whispered frantically from inside. "I hear something."

Curtis knocked lightly before pushing his way inside. "We've come to help."

"Go on now," a woman scolded. "We don't need no help. Men have done enough."

Maura stepped past him into the one-room home. Three women kneeled on the floor around Hazel. They'd made a bed out of old blankets. One stroked Hazel's head while holding a bowl of liquid. The two others, one in pale green and the other in brown, held down Hazel's legs.

"We've come to help Hazel," Maura stated. The humidity made it hard to breathe. She stared at the scene, not knowing what to do. She felt her magick calling forth power from the surrounding landscape, urging her to freeze everyone to make the moment stop. The panic wasn't helpful.

"There's nothing you can do, ma'am," the woman by Hazel's head answered. "Please don't trouble yourself."

"Not after what was done," the woman in a faded green dress added under her breath.

"Margaret," the woman next to her admonished.

"Ida," Margaret mimicked Ida's tone.

"Less talk," the woman holding Hazel's head ordered.

"Curtis, fan the door, see if we can't get some air in here," Maura directed.

Ida stood and rushed past Curtis to stop him. She jerked the door from his hands and slammed it shut. "Best not let the night spirits in."

Hazel screamed, her whole body tensing.

"Shh." The woman placed her hand over Hazel's mouth, but it did little to stop the sound. "Sun'll be up soon enough, and then you can make all the noise you want."

Maura took a deep breath. These women clearly knew more about what to do than she did. As a warlock, human medicine wasn't exactly her forte. If anything serious happened to a warlock, there was usually a magickal solution on hand.

"Ya know about what happened to her, by who?" Maura asked.

The women glanced at each other, but only Ida nodded.

"Then ya know about things that are..." Maura wasn't sure how to explain it. She lifted her hand and rubbed the tips to make them glow like she had to read the letters. It was a simple trick, but it got her point across. The women gasped. "I'm here to help."

Maura kneeled by Hazel's head and whispered an incantation to calm her before taking away her voice to stop the sound of her screams. It didn't stop her pain, but it kept the cries from echoing.

"Who are you?" Ida asked. "A witch?"

"Warlock, actually," Maura answered. Hazel stared at her with dazed eyes. "Maura MacGregor."

"She's a friend," Curtis assured the women. "A good spirit."

"I'd give anything for an attending and an epidural," Maura mumbled to herself as she touched Hazel's head.

"I have the caudle," the woman offered her bowl of liquid.

Ida stared at Curtis's clothes. "Where you from, boy?"

"We came across a ghost army marching

backward. It carried us from the future and led us here," Curtis answered.

Maura arched a brow at him, unsure more honesty was the best policy at the moment.

He shrugged.

"I think I know how all those old ghost stories ya heard as a child got started." Maura placed her hands on Hazel's stomach. She had no clue what she was doing, but she focused her magick and hoped for the best. She concentrated on easing Hazel's suffering.

Suddenly bright lights burst from Maura's fingertips. She gasped, surprised by the surge of power flowing through her. The stomach lost its firmness. A baby began to cry.

"Blessed!" Ida exclaimed, falling back in surprise. She'd caught the baby in her arms.

Curtis quickly darted forward to take the baby as Ida rolled onto her back. He lifted the child from her arms. Maura stood, reaching to examine the baby.

"Is she—"

A bright light flashed like a camera strobe the second she bumped Curtis's arm.

"Maura? What's going on? What are ya doing here so early?"

Maura blinked in confusion. "Ma?"

They stood in the front reception hall of the

MacGregor mansion. White marble floors, a wide staircase with a hand-carved oak railing, and the giant crystal chandelier could not have contrasted the small cabin more. This mansion had never been Maura's home. The family had only owned it for a handful of years. Though beautiful, it seemed ostentatious, like a Georgian-style palace that would be better suited as a museum.

"Who's your friends?" Cait MacGregor had the annoying habit of never looking out of sorts. By the light coming in the window, dawn peeked over the horizon. Somehow her mother still managed to be dressed like the cover of a 1950s high-end catalog, pearls and all, at the early hour. Not a single hair was out of its perfect place.

Maura glanced down. Her t-shirt was dirty, and she smelled of sweat and horse. Any makeup that hadn't rubbed off was probably smeared.

Curtis stood next to her. He looked exhausted and more than a little confused. He'd wrapped the edge of his shirt over the naked baby as she cried in his arms.

"Maura?" her ma insisted. "Manners. Introduce me."

"Oh, uh, Curtis, this is my ma, Cait MacGregor," Maura introduced. "Ma, this is Curtis Jefferson, owner of Crimson Tavern, and this is his grandmother."

"Very droll, my daughter." Cait swiped her hand to direct Maura to stand aside. Her welcoming smile dropped when she came closer to the baby. "This is a fresh, sweet one. Maura, did ya—?"

"Easy, ma, you're not a grandmother yet," Maura answered.

"Where's her mother?" Cait asked.

"1864, thereabouts," Curtis said.

Cait frowned as she waited for the punchline.

"Och, there's a wee bairn!" Raibeart MacGregor stood on the balcony above the front hall, looking down on them. He was dressed like a member of King Louis XIV's royal court in bouffant breeches, a white silk shirt, white gloves, and a plumed hat. The feather bounced as he sauntered toward the steps.

"Maura Mary Margareta MacGregor! What kind of wicked magick have ya been dabbling in?" Cait demanded as she reached for the newborn. She paused, looking at the back of Curtis's hand before taking the baby.

The red heels of Raibeart's buckled shoes clacked on the marble floor. One of his silk stockings had fallen off his calf and pooled around his ankle.

"I didn't do anything," Maura protested. "It was done to us."

Cait cradled the baby in her arms, not seeming to care that the baby ruined her silk blouse. "Nothing? Ya show up with a baby out of time, and this one," she nodded at Curtis, "reeks of vampire ash."

"Maura had nothing to do with that." Curtis stepped forward as if he meant to protect her. "I killed the vampire. Any fate that comes of it is mine. Not hers."

Cait hummed softly, and Maura saw her mother hide a small smile. She started walking away with the baby.

"Um, Maura? Did your mother just confiscate my mawmaw?" Curtis asked, moving to follow Cait.

Maura touched his arm to stop him.

"She's a healer. Better than a doctor. She knows what she's doing." Maura watched Abigail's tiny arms flail. "Ma, we need ya to check the baby. I didn't know what to do."

Cait hummed softly as she carried the baby toward the dining room.

Raibeart tried to intercede. "I got her."

Cait dodged his hands as he attempted to take the baby from her. "First things, first. Raibeart, we need supplies—clothes, formula, and diapers. This baby is counting on ya."

"Aye." Raibeart nodded, taking on the mission.

"What's this sweet one's name?" Cait asked.

"Abigail," Curtis said.

"Formula, diapers, unicorn onesie, tricycle." Raibeart strode for the front door.

"Clothes, formula, diapers, no contraptions," Cait yelled from the dining room. "She's a newborn, not a toy."

Raibeart scoffed and said to Maura, "The tricycle is for Bridgette." Then, as he touched the doorknob, he yelled, "Euann, I'm taking your car!"

"Is your uncle going to go out like that?" Curtis pointed after Raibeart.

"At least he's wearing clothes," Maura said, unconcerned.

"Who's Bridgette?" he asked.

"No clue." Maura suppressed a yawn. "I don't know about ya, but I'm exhausted. That was one hell of a night. My family will make sure Abigail is safe."

"She is my family, my responsibility," Curtis rubbed his eye and yawned. "I'll take care of her."

"We need rest if we're going even to begin to unpack what happened last night. My ma is better than a doctor. Abigail is in good hands." Maura pointed toward the dining room. "They have plenty of room for guests. We'll be safe here."

"I have a cot at the restaurant. I can crash there," Curtis said. "I need to make sure the restaurant got locked up."

Maura didn't want him to leave. "This house is magickally protected. Vampires and their minions wouldn't dare come here looking for ya."

Curtis looked too tired to protest. He suppressed another yawn. "It won't be an imposition?"

Maura smiled. She went through the dining room, past the long wood dining table. The sound of running water and her mother singing came from the kitchen beyond. "Ma, it's been a long night. We're going to take a room."

Cait had the baby cradled in one arm as she ran water in the sink to clean the newborn. "Shower before dinner. Ya look terrible."

"Yeah, no imposition." Maura laughed softly. To her mother, she asked, "Ya all right if we leave Abigail with ya?"

Cait arched a brow at the stupid question.

"Oh and have someone check on the Crimson Tavern to make sure the waitress locked the doors last night." Maura yawned. "Please?"

"Consider it done," Cait said.

Maura led the way through the kitchen.

Curtis didn't readily follow. "How is she?"

"Sweet as an angel," Cait answered. "Ten fingers. Ten toes. One nose."

"Since I'm still alive, does that mean we get her back where she belongs?" he asked.

"Unless ya fractured some timelines or are stuck in some kind of loop." Cait kept her voice soft as she continued to wash the baby. "Go rest. We'll get Abigail settled, and I'll confer with the other elders. See if we can't patch up any holes in the natural order."

Curtis reached into his pocket and pulled out the letters. He looked at Maura, who nodded that he should give them to her mother. He set them down on the counter. "I don't know if this will help, but we found them tonight. Thank you for your kindness, Mrs. MacGregor."

"See that, Maura? The boy has manners. Ya could learn a thing or two from your handsome friend," Cait said.

Chapter Six

Curtis stared at the large painting of Maura dominating a wall of the bedroom as he listened to the sound of the shower coming from the en suite. Though the portrait looked like it came from the Victorian era, Maura's face appeared precisely the same as if age had not touched her. He would have assumed it was a novelty if not for the fact warlocks were immortal unless murdered.

The bedroom reminded him of luxury spa advertisements. White painted walls contrasted the dark wood of the oversized furniture. Thick tapestry curtains blocked the light from outside but for a beam of light coming through the opening.

"I've always hated that portrait," Maura grumbled.

"I think it's beautiful." Curtis turned to look at her.

Maura wore a long silky nightgown. Her red hair had been slicked back from her face. She'd insisted he took the first shower while she found him a pair of sweatpants and a t-shirt that belonged to a cousin.

"I hate what that portrait represents. My brothers would say what I'm about to do is called a tirade," she warned.

"By all means, rant away," Curtis said, completely enamored with her.

She didn't need much invitation. "All right. In my family, the men act like women are delicate flowers who they need to keep safe. Then my mother insists that I act like a lady. Have ya ever tried to pelt gremians with energy balls through white gloves? There is not enough bleach on Earth to get that stain out. And don't get me started on running in heels and a corset."

Maura inhaled a deep breath.

"My ma keeps trying to convince me to grow my hair out like that picture. And watch…" Maura conjured a fireball in her hand and threw it at the portrait.

Curtis stepped back in surprise. The magick sizzled and disappeared, leaving the painting intact.

"Indestructible. Every time we move, that monstrosity shows up in my bedroom. I keep telling her it was a different time." Maura ran her fingers through her hair, pulling at the strands to show the length. "Ya don't have to have long hair and ballgowns to be a lady."

Curtis smiled.

She sighed. "OK. Rant over. Thanks for listening. Sorry, I'm so tired and grouchy."

"I like how you have your hair." Curtis liked a lot of things about this woman. She had a kind smile and gentle voice but also showed confidence and bravery in the face of danger. Most people liked to think they'd be brave if tested, but the truth was not many people would face an 1860s colony ruled over by vampires. Maura hadn't hesitated. "I thought you lived at the motel."

"I do." Maura sighed. "I can't tell ya how grateful I was when the family assigned me to take over Hotel Motel because it meant I wouldn't be expected to live here in the family mansion. This place may be huge, but there is absolutely no privacy."

"How many people stay here?"

Maura yawned and gave a dainty shrug. "Um, my parents, Uncle Raibeart, Uncle Angus and Aunt Margareta, Uncle Fergus and his new wife Donna when they're not traveling. Angus' children all have rooms here. Kenneth lives here with his new wife and his daughter, who is six. Aunt Margareta probably wouldn't let him leave even if he wanted to. She is all about being a grandma. My twin brothers, Rory and Bruce, though Bruce technically lives at the motel too."

"That's right, the brother who paints obscene pictures on the motel walls." Curtis put his hand over his mouth to suppress a yawn.

"Ya must be exhausted." She yawned the words as she spoke and gestured at the bed. "Ya can have this one. I'll find another."

"This bed is big enough for ten of us." Curtis pulled the covers back and collapsed onto the high mattress.

Maura followed suit, crawling up before rolling on top of the gold comforter. Her arms dropped to her sides, and she didn't move. "How's your stab wound? I forgot to ask ma to check it."

"Sore. Fine. I don't care." Curtis closed his eyes.

Somewhere in exhausted sleep, he felt energy calling to him. It lingered like an orb floating through his consciousness, weaving in and out of fragmented dreams. When he finally opened his eyes, he felt as if the night in the Mississippi countryside had to have been an illusion.

That didn't explain why he awoke in a luxurious mansion or why Maura MacGregor lay next to him with her hand firmly intertwined with his, fingers tangled together. Her eyes were open, sleepily staring at him as if they'd woken at the same time.

Curtis did not have moments like this in life. He didn't date much. With so many secrets, it was hard to let people get close to him. Instead, he concentrated on work and providing for Abigail.

"What do ya want out of life? Don't think, just answer," Maura whispered. A soft light came through the window, adding to the intimacy of the moment.

"To not be a dhampir." The admission surprised him. That was not something he could change. "How about you?"

"I don't know anymore." Maura inched closer. "I feel like I stopped knowing around the time that my ma commissioned that portrait to be painted."

"What did you want?" Curtis liked the smell of her shampoo, lavender with a hint of tea tree. He only knew that much because he'd been in the shower before her.

Maura laughed. "I don't remember an exact thing, but there were things I was excited to try and learn. I ran the MacGregor stables for a time. I seduced a king to stop a war. That was fun. I—"

"You slept with a king?" Curtis frowned,

finding himself strangely jealous without reason to be.

"No, seduced him, didn't have sex with him." Maura laughed. "Royalty is too easy. Kings can never imagine that someone might not be in awe of them. I find it a disgusting trait."

Curtis felt her fingers moving against his. Each tiny caress sent a shiver of awareness through him. "I don't think people are in awe of me."

Maura laughed harder. "That is either the best or the worst pickup line I've ever heard."

"I was going for best." Curtis grinned.

The energy he felt in his dreams stirred between them, drawing him closer. He didn't think as he leaned in for a kiss. The soft press of her mouth made him forget everything else. He slid his fingers away from her hand and cupped her cheek.

"Maura…"

The sound came from far away. He deepened the kiss.

"Oh, Maura…"

The voice was closer. Maura made a weak noise against his mouth.

Curtis pulled away and looked around the room. "Ghost?"

Maura frowned. "Worse. Cousins."

"Oh, Maura…" Two men spoke in unison,

singing her name like taunting schoolchildren. Loud pounding erupted on the door, followed by laughter.

"We know you're in there!"

"Go away, Euann," Maura yelled.

"Come out and play with us. We want to meet your new friend!"

"Go away, Iain!" Maura sighed and pushed up from the bed.

Curtis didn't want to let her go, but he didn't have a choice. The feel of her kiss lingered on his mouth.

"Don't ya have wives to harass?" Maura called.

"Jane's landscaping the new city garden," Iain said.

"Cora's busy with the library remodel," Euann added. "Come on, Maura. Let us in. We miss ya."

"Do ya ever think your wives take on all these extra projects to get away from ya dunderheads?" Maura teased. To Curtis, she said, "Yeah, sorry, they're not going to leave. I told ya. No privacy in the mansion."

He stood next to the bed and began pulling up the sheets. Maura saw what he was trying to do and swiped her hand through the air. Magick glistened over the bed. The sheets and comforter straightened themselves.

"We want to meet your boyfriend," Euann said. Tiny yellow sparks came from under the doorframe, followed by laughter. "Open up."

Maura gathered his clothes from the night before and shook them out. Blue lights glimmered over them before she tossed them on the bed. "Those are clean if ya want to change."

She went to her dresser and tugged a pair of slacks on under her nightgown. Curtis politely averted his gaze as they finished dressing.

"Maura, oh, Maura…"

Curtis heard her go to the bedroom door and take a deep breath.

She glanced at him, mumbling, "I'm so sorry about everything that is about to happen."

Maura opened the door, and a hand holding a cup of coffee appeared instantly from the hallway.

"Thought ya might need this," Iain said, pushing his way inside. He held a second cup. Seeing Curtis, he grinned and offered the coffee. "And this."

Curtis nodded his thanks and began to take a sip. Maura sniffed her cup and shoved it against Iain. Hot liquid sloshed against him, and he cried out in protest. She batted the mug out of Curtis's hand. Coffee spilled on the floor, soaking into the carpet.

"Seriously? Truth potion?" Maura grimaced.

Euann and Iain tried to look innocent and failed. There was an unmistakable family resemblance between Maura and her cousins. Whatever dominant gene flowed in the MacGregor family was a strong one.

"Is that what that was?" Euann asked Iain. "I thought it said creamer."

"Aunt Cait must have mixed up the labels again," Iain answered.

"I'm going to tell Aunt Margareta that ya were in the family potions again," Maura threatened.

"There's no need to be dramatic." Iain shared a look with his brother.

"Honest mistake." Euann couldn't be bothered to hide his smirk.

"Follow me, Curtis." Maura pushed past her cousins as they blocked the door. "I'll find us real coffee."

Curtis tried to follow her, but Iain and Euann stepped close to each other to block his way. He didn't feel comfortable shoving the men aside in their own home.

Curtis had met both men before at the Crimson Tavern. At the time, Iain had glamoured Euann's face to hide the fact his brother had been stuck shifted somewhere between human and fox. The locals didn't know about the paranormal or magick, and the supernatural community was generally happy to leave it that way. It was probably one of the only things they all agreed upon with little argument.

"How's it going, barkeep?" Euann asked. Thankfully the man's fox face had returned to normal. Still, knowing the man had the power to change into an animal was disconcerting.

"Fine?" Curtis ducked to move past them.

"Ya know, we have to ask." Iain crossed his arms and blocked the escape attempt.

"Ya are staying in our house. It's a matter of family duty," Euann added.

Curtis took a step back, not liking their serious expressions. He was ready to fight if he had to, even if he was no match against shifter warlocks and their magick.

"My intentions with your cousin are honorable," Curtis stated. "I would never take advantage of—"

"Maura?" Euann laughed. "We're not worried about her. The last man who messed with her ended up—well, we don't talk about poor Rodney."

Iain put his hand against his chest and bowed his head, whispering, "Poor Rodney."

"Iain! Euann! Leave him be!" Maura yelled from what sounded like the direction of the kitchen.

"I'm confused." Curtis frowned, looking from one warlock to the other and back again. "What then is a matter of duty? Is this about Abigail?"

"We need to know if you're dating Maura, does that mean…" Euann glanced at Iain, who gestured for him to keep talking.

"Mean?" Curtis prompted. He wanted this conversation to be over. The last thing he needed was to worry about Maura's cousins. He had Abigail the time-traveling baby, and a den of psychotic vampires to worry about.

"Since you're dating Maura, does that mean we get a family discount on those tater tot nachos?" Euann asked.

"Though, probably don't tell her about this Abigail lady," Iain said, again holding his heart and bowing his head. "Poor Rodney."

"Aye, Rodney," Euann mimicked Iain's mournful tone.

Curtis wasn't sure if he should laugh. "Are you serious—*nachos*?"

"*Tater tot* nachos," Euann clarified. "Our women say they're life changing, and we like our women happy."

"Uh, yeah, sure, I'll give ya a discount next time ya come in." Curtis's business ran on very thin profit margins, so he was careful not to commit to lifetime discounts. It wasn't like the MacGregor family needed to clip coupons.

"My man," Euann exclaimed, slapping Curtis on the arm before gripping his bicep. "But make sure ya treat Maura nicely. We'd hate to have to hurt the nacho man."

Curtis weakly nodded. He was too tired to engage in this kind of tomfoolery for much longer.

"We've been meaning to ask." Iain slung his arm around his shoulders and led him out of the bedroom. "Have ya given any thought to adding some Scottish dishes to the menu? I know it's an English pub, but it could be a Scottish one which is vastly superior. Think about it."

"We're more of a Southern cuisine place," Curtis answered. "Burgers, beer, catfish, and I've been thinking of maybe organizing an old-fash-ioned crawdad boil. Up in Door County, they do the fish boil with whitefish that brings in tourists every year. I thought maybe I'd start a new tradi-tion for Green Vallis."

"Have ya ever had haggis?" Euann asked.

"Cullen skink and Scotch pies?" Iain added.

"Maybe you should start a festival," Curtis suggested. "Invite true Scottish chefs to do it right."

Curtis wasn't too worried that promises of

haggis would lure away his burger and beer Wisconsin customers.

"Just think about it." Iain let go of him as they reached the kitchen. He and Euann exited into the dining room.

"Think about what?" Maura asked, bringing Curtis a fresh cup of coffee. "Cream? Sugar?"

"Sugar," Curtis answered. Maura turned and went back to the counter to put sugar in one of the cups. "And, uh, they had some questions about the menu. Hey, have you seen your mother and Abigail?"

"They'll be around here somewhere. Don't worry. My ma was born to take care of babies." She stirred his coffee before carrying it into the dining room for him. "So, what kind of questions?"

"Adding some Scottish dishes to the menu. Silken Stink, something like that."

"Silken…?" Maura placed the cup on the wood table, unconcerned with the wood finish. She started to laugh. "Cullen skink?"

"That's the one," he said. "But I think I'm going to stick to what I know. I'm not even sure what that is."

"Creamy fish soup," Maura went back into the kitchen and came back with a tray of pastries and napkins. "Are ya hungry?"

"Not for fish soup."

Maura laughed.

He sat next to her at the formal dining room table. "I'm debating on whether or not I call my mawmaw to tell her what's happening. I don't want her to worry, but it does involve her."

"We don't know what's happening," Maura pointed out. She took a big bite out of a cheese Danish before setting it on her napkin. "And we don't know if or when we'll be going back."

A sense of urgency filled him. Last time they'd traveled without warning.

"I was thinking, maybe we pack some supplies and be ready in case the ghost army comes for us." Curtis took a sticky bun and ate it in two bites. Who knew where they'd find themselves if it happened again? He grabbed a nut-covered cinnamon roll and wrapped it in a napkin. "I should find Abigail. She needs to be with us. She's too little to time travel on her own."

"You're right." Maura stood. "Let's get her."

Curtis put his hand on her wrist as she reached for her danish. "About this morning."

Her smile caused his breath to catch. Even now, he wanted to kiss her.

"To be continued." She nodded that he should follow her. "First things first."

He made it two steps before the room began

to tremble. Coffee cups danced along the surface as the table vibrated.

"Earthquake." Curtis grabbed Maura by the arm and tugged her into the entryway for protection. He wrapped his arms around her and tucked her head against his chest. "Don't move. Everything'll be all right."

Chapter Seven

Maura's senses tingled as Curtis pressed her against the entryway. It wasn't just the awareness of his body, which was marvelous, but the tingling in her magick. This was no ordinary earthquake. Like the storm that came the night before, this event of nature did not bode well.

The sound of cracking stone erupted in the front hall. She pulled on his arm to get a look at what was happening. The marble floor popped to create little broken mountains across the once-flat surface.

"To the enchanted forest," Raibeart yelled from the top balcony. The sound of a laughing toddler followed the call. "They'll never find us there."

The shaking continued. Trees burst through

the tops of the marble mountains, growing tall over the hall. Dust shook from the leaves as they spun into existence.

"What the——?" Curtis's body remained locked into place, shielding her.

"Jewel," Maura answered, lightly tapping his arm to urge him to free her. "My little cousin is quite powerful and apparently under the influence of the questionable judgment of Uncle Raibeart. Again."

The trees blocked the view of the balcony and left only enough room for narrow stone paths. Curtis slowly reached to touch one of the trunks. "How is this…?"

"Raibeart, ya bring that baby back here," Cait demanded.

"Let's hide from the evil queen," Raibeart answered. "Run, Jewel, run!"

Jewel screamed with laughter at the game.

Maura stepped into the trees and tried to weave her way toward the stairs. A blur of movement slid past her. Jewel's magick had turned the stairway into a slide. Raibeart held Abigail in a baby sling against his chest as they escaped into the forest.

"Raibeart," Maura called. "Stop. We——"

"Jewel, quick, stop the evil princess!" Raibeart yelled.

Jewel laughed. A tree slid in front of Maura to block her path. Curtis bumped into her as they came to an abrupt stop.

"What is happening?" Curtis asked.

Maura changed directions, but the trees kept moving to block their way. Finally stopping, she hit the flat of her hand against a trunk in frustration. "Jewel is a phoenix. Raibeart must have taken off her binding bracelet so she could tap into her powers."

The familiar sound of drums began in the dining room. Fear knotted her stomach. Maura gripped Curtis's arm and tried to navigate through the moving trees. Jewel was only six and very sheltered. She would think this a fun game and wouldn't understand the danger.

"Raibeart," Maura yelled, panicking as their path continued to be blocked. "We need ya to give us Abigail!"

Jewel's laughter echoed over them. Curtis pushed at the tree trunks in a failed attempt to dislodge them.

"Raibeart, I'm not playing around." Maura switched directions. She stumbled over the torn-up marble floor. More trees moved to create a wall between them and the children. The drums were joined by marching feet. The sound began to echo all around them. Maura grabbed Curtis's arm. "Ghost army."

He pulled her against his chest, and they braced themselves.

"Raibeart, protect those babies!" Maura cried.

The trees retracted into the floor, but it was too late. The drummer boy was upon them, leading the soldiers in their backward march. Maura caught sight of Raibeart kneeling on the ground holding the two girls. A pink forcefield with tiny yellow flowers emanated from Jewel.

The drummer reached them. Icy shards pierced her insides like the time before. Curtis grunted in surprise at the sudden pain as the drummer affected him too. Light flashed, and the drumbeats stopped.

They gasped for breath, clinging to each other and fighting the chill of the ghost's touch. They were back on the Mississippi plantation. Evening light spread over the slave quarters, the last stretches of sun before darkness would claim the earth. The sound of doors slamming shut rever- berated around them.

"Abigail?" Curtis asked, frantically looking around. "Do you see her? Did she come back with us?"

"She's not here," Maura assured him.

"Raibeart and Jewel were able to protect her. I saw them right before we were transported."

"But—"

Maura touched his arm. "Trust me. Jewel is the most powerful creature I've ever seen. If she were old enough to control her powers, she probably could have brought us back and forth through time at will."

Unfortunately, Jewel was only six. Her understanding of complex magick was finding ways to materialize cookies from the kitchen after her grandma told her she couldn't have anymore.

"Everyone's hiding again," Maura observed. "No one's outside."

Lights shone through holes in the nearby cabins in a soft glistening firelight, but the flickers went undisturbed as if those inside were too afraid to move and cast shadows. Insects serenaded the late hour. The constant hum of their song enhanced the stillness.

Tiny vibrations ran up her arm from where she touched him. She wanted to tell him that everything was all right, that she wasn't scared. That would have been a lie. She was terrified of what these trips into the past might mean.

"Maura?" He touched her cheek.

"We're going to get through this," she whispered, wishing she sounded more confident.

"Vampires are near," he stated.

Maura nodded. She felt them too. "What are we doing back at this place? Abigail has already been born. What more can we do here?"

"Listen. If they find us, I want you to save yourself." His thumb ran along her cheek before his fingers cupped the side of her head, forcing her to look at him. He appeared as if he wanted to kiss her but held back. "This is my family tree, my past. Whatever dark magick is messing with us, it should have never brought you here. You're in danger because of me. Promise me. If it goes bad, you'll do whatever you need to save yourself. It's me they are mad at."

Maura would promise no such thing. "I'm not running, and I am not leaving ya."

"Yes, you are, Maura."

"Only if you're running with me, Curtis." She put her hand over his, keeping him pressed against her face. "And if there is a fight, we fight together. Maybe we were both brought back for a reason. Maybe you're supposed to help your ancestors be free of this, and I'm supposed to help ya."

He shook his head in denial. "If that were true, if we had come back in time and succeeded, I would have had a very different childhood."

Her heart pounded. The vibrations became more insistent, drawing her closer to him. She'd had this feeling before, tucked away in the depths of her nightmares. In the middle of all the pain and blood and fear, this feeling had been there to quietly center her. Until now, she'd never known what it could be.

"Fucking time travel," Maura swore.

"Fucking time travel," Curtis agreed.

His mouth pressed against hers in a stirring kiss. She grabbed his face, keeping him next to her. Danger only added to their resolve to capture this moment, this feeling brewing between them.

His hands slid to her waist, and part of her wanted to tear at his shirt, unmindful of where they were.

Suddenly, the insects stopped. Curtis pulled away from her and clutched his stomach as if he were about to be sick. Her lips protested the loss of contact.

"I have a bad feeling about this," he said.

The high-pitched screech of a mythical creature sounded in the darkening sky. Maura had never heard such a beast.

Curtis gripped her arm and began pulling her with him. "I know that cry. We have to hide."

Maura stumbled with him toward the nearby trees. "Curt—"

"Shh," he urged.

Maura watched the sky.

"Interesting. I was not told we were expecting visitors tonight."

They stopped short of the trees. She searched the shadows along the tree line but didn't see who spoke. Her magick tried to surge forth, but she held it back, not wanting to give away her powers. Her family wasn't here for magickal support, and she had no idea how many they'd be up against. Vampire dens could have dozens of members.

The last traces of dusk dissipated into the night sky.

They didn't move, didn't speak. More voices came from the trees.

"Two lost lambs."

"Ready for the slaughter."

"I'm a might bit peckish."

"Quiet!" A cowboy stepped out of the trees. Long stringy hair hung over his shoulders beneath a weathered hat. His stance was deceptively easygoing as he strolled toward them. His eyes glowed with an inner light, and he didn't even try to hide his fangs.

"Virgile," Curtis whispered, spooked.

"From the...?" Maura didn't finish the sentence. Virgile did not need to know about his future death.

"Have we met?" Virgile asked, a cruel smile crossing his corpselike features. "Did I eat your family? I'm sorry I don't remember. I admit I dine on many families." He pointed at Maura. "Though you are someone that I would remember. Your smell is not quite human."

Maura glanced over the trees and took an involuntary step back.

Virgile laughed and put his hands on his hips. Mocking, he asked, "Did someone conjure a witch?"

The vampire darted forward, so fast his movements were a blur. When he stopped, he stood behind Maura.

"Let her—" Curtis charged but didn't make it more than a step before Virgile sent him flying backward.

On reflex, magick flowed from deep within Maura. It shot from her hand to cushion Curtis's fall. Curtis landed on the ground with a solid *thunk*.

"Oh, you're not just an ordinary naked moon dancer, are you?" Virgile grabbed her wrists tight. "You've got real power."

More than a dozen vampires revealed themselves from within the trees, three dressed like cowboys, but most appeared to be soldiers. Their eyes glistened with the same eerie light.

Curtis surged from the ground, angling his shoulder to ram Virgile's waist. "Let her go!"

Virgile darted to the side, jerking Maura as he kneed Curtis in the face. Blood sprayed from Curtis's mouth, and he was again flung to the ground. Instantly the vampires were on him like rabid dogs on raw meat. They pinned him to the ground.

Maura let her magick loose. She sent a wave over the vampires, sending them sprawling in all directions. They quickly caught themselves and darted to Curtis once more. Curtis cried out in pain and anger as he flung his arms and legs to kick them off. More of the creatures emerged from the trees.

"Stop!" Virgile ordered.

The vampires instantly obeyed, crawling back from Curtis lying on the ground. They stared with resentment at the one who commanded them.

"What are you?" Virgile demanded, sniffing the air. "You're not a vampire."

Claw marks bled on Curtis's arms, showing through his ripped shirt, but she couldn't tell if he'd been bitten.

Energy hummed inside Maura. Her fear caused her magick to draw power from the nearby forest. Trees withered and died, drained of life as they fueled her.

"Curtis, stay down!" Maura yelled. She sent another surge at the attackers. They flung back only to find their footing and return. Virgile was forced to release her, but he returned seconds later to renew his hold.

Maura did it again, killing more trees and using her magick to push Virgile away. She flung balls of magick at random targets. Some vampires screeched in pain but recovered. Only a few exploded into death flames. Those would have been the newly turned. The older vampires were too strong for thrusts of magick to do much damage. The virus inside them had survived and mutated for centuries, making them immune to Maura's powers.

Virgile did not return. She readied another energy ball. A high-pitched whistle caught her attention. She turned to find a vampire had a blade pressed against Curtis's throat. Blood trickled from a shallow cut.

This vampire wasn't like the others. Dark brown hair was streaked with gray at the temples. He emanated death and staring into his eyes was like looking into the milky stare of a corpse. The cowboys and soldiers instantly laid themselves on the ground, prostrate before their vampire king. His long blue coat appeared as if it came from the old country, embroidered along the edges with elaborate gold stitching.

Curtis's eyes met hers as if trying to convey a

message. His lips moved, mouthing the word, "Run."

Maura refused. She would not leave him.

"Interesting." King Vampire didn't sound like the locals indicating her first assumption of him coming from the old country was correct. He sounded of the Baltic region. "You smell of my blood."

Buford?

Maura frowned. Not to pre-judge, but this vampire did not look like a Buford. She would have pegged him for a Vlad Dracula.

"Let him go," Maura commanded, trying to distract him. She lifted her hand in warning, holding a ball of swirling blue lights.

The vampire's eyes moved over Maura. "And you use the primitive magick of a warlock. Put your toy down, little girl."

She really wanted to throw it at him.

"Ah." Buford pointed the blade at Curtis's heart in a warning. "I said down."

Maura threw the energy to her side, unable to resist grazing the backs of two prone vampires. One of them burst into flames. Buford chuckled as if she were a naughty child throwing a tantrum and not a real supernatural threat.

"Would you be one of the MacGregor

warlocks?" Buford asked, slowly returning the knife to Curtis's neck.

Maura didn't answer.

The old vampire tilted his head. "The accent gave it away. You're either a MacGregor or a MacIntyre." Buford didn't take his eyes off her. "See if she's alone."

The vampires pushed up from the ground and scattered like blurs in the night until only Virgile and Buford remained. Maura tried to calculate how much power she'd have to drain from the surrounding nature to create enough magick to stun Buford and free Curtis. The old vampire's eyes dared her to try.

Moonlight and clouds caused the shadows to shift over the landscape. Silence lay eerily over the countryside. Not even the hum of insects broke through as if they hid in their homes and endeavored not to be detected by the lurking evil.

A bruise formed on Curtis's cheek. Blood trailed down his neck. His ripped shirt hung in tatters on his shoulders. The vampires' attack had shredded the material. Despite that, his eyes were clear, and his chest heaved for breath as if he held back the urge to fight.

"I hear your heart." Buford lifted Curtis's wrist and licked a wound on his arm. Tasting the blood, he recoiled and spat it out as if burned. "What are you? You taste like rot."

Curtis refused to answer.

"Virgile, escort our guest," Buford ordered.

Curtis grunted as Buford lifted him into the air, kicking and fighting to be free. The knife dropped to the ground, embedding hilt deep in the dirt.

Maura reacted, trying to run after them to stop Curtis's capture. She barely made it one step before Virgile had hold of her arms from behind. He hoisted her into the air. Nails bit into her flesh.

Maura cried out, terrified as he carried her over the roofs of the cabins. Unlike her cousin, Iain, she did not have the ability to shift into a bird if the vampire dropped her. They sped over the landscape. Virgile let loose an earsplitting screech, a call of warning to all those below to fear the night.

Her body jerked as he flung her wildly. She kicked her legs in a pointless attempt to find footing where there was none. Nausea threatened her stomach, and she screamed.

In that moment of complete physical fear, her body reacted, pulling energy from anything and everything living. A green fog came from the treetops, flooding her body. She felt the life of animals and people and instantly tried to force those energies back. She did not want to live off the misfortune of others, even if it was to save herself.

Virgile dove toward the ground. Her legs hit the dirt. The vampire dragged her several yards before letting go. Maura clutched handfuls of dirt and grass, trying to hold on to the solid feel beneath her. The grass withered in her hands. Dizzy, she wove back and forth as her head swam. She attempted to crawl.

"Curtis," she tried to yell his name, but it came out on a croak.

Torches threw light over the yard. Her hands glowed with blue. Magick tingled its way up her arm. The power was too much, too hard to control.

Virgile strode past her. She watched claws retract into his hands, and the features from a bat shift disappear into his face. He stepped onto the porch of a two-story plantation house.

Thick white columns supported the covered porch and upper deck, framing the large rectangular doors and windows. She saw tiny movements in the curtains. People watched from inside but were too scared to reveal themselves. The white paint and picture-perfect look of the big house were a stark contrast to the cabins.

Virgile joined Buford on the porch. They

watched her, arms crossed and curious. Curtis lay motionless at their feet.

Every instinct told her to eject her magick at the vampires and end their reign of terror. No one would blame her—no one that mattered. She could blow them and this whole damned place off the map.

But to end the vampires meant to kill Curtis, to hurt the unknown people peeking out at her.

Did she kill less than a dozen innocents to save the lives of many?

Could she hurt Curtis?

The magick burned like lava in her veins.

Loud thuds dropped like fat rain onto the ground as vampires landed in perfect formation over the yard. She recognized some of the cowboys from outside the cabins, but most were uniformed soldiers. Buford did not have a den. He had an army.

The sound of dropping feet became too numerous to count. Maura fought for control as she tried to find her footing. One of the vampires landed closer to her, and she jerked back to escape their nearness.

The moment she stood, she heard the familiar drumming of the ghost army, only this time they weren't ghosts. The drummer boy tatted on his drums. His eyes fixated on her neck. His lips parted, and he snarled as if he wanted nothing more than to bite her. Buford had turned a thirteen-year-old boy.

"No. Stop. I want to watch what she does," Buford said. He pressed his hand to Virgile's chest to stop him mid-movement.

Maura did not want to turn her back on the vampire army, but everywhere she looked, they had surrounded her.

Curtis had regained consciousness. He stared at her, mouthing her name, telling her what looked like to run. Buford pressed his boot into the man's back.

She felt her hair lifting off her head. Her skin began to crackle, the lava painfully bubbling to the surface.

At that moment, she knew all she had to do was let go. Magick would pulse out of her like a nuclear weapon, taking out both the army and their king. It would burn the plantation house and surrounding grounds, erasing the ugliness from the earth. She could end the suffering, stop generations of Buford's terror.

She knew Curtis would tell her to stop Buford at any cost, even his life. She knew because that is what she would ask him to do if their roles were reversed.

Her control started to slip. Light shot out of

her chest, striking a soldier. The vampire screeched and took off into the air in a ball of flames. A second wayward blast erupted from her knee. A third was expelled from her hand. Each release felt like death.

"I'm sorry," Maura whispered to Curtis.

She couldn't hold on.

Maura lifted her arms. Her body levitated from the ground. When the magick left her, it pierced through her skin in glassy shards. It left her eyes, her mouth, her ears. It burst from her chest.

Death screeches filled the night as the morbid fireworks of burning vampires shot over the yard.

When all the magick had been expelled, Maura dropped to her hands and knees. The drummer boy turned into embers, then ash. His drum dropped to the ground, rolling toward her hand.

A single clap sounded from the plantation home. She looked to the side. The army was gone, but the king and his head lackey remained in front of their plantation castle. In the end, she couldn't sacrifice Curtis or those within the home.

Maura watched Buford's boots loom toward her. He kicked the drum out of his way before kneeling.

"That was an impressive display," Buford said, pushing a strand of her hair behind her ear.

She jerked her head away, the only defiance she could muster.

"Bring him." Buford motioned toward the porch.

Virgile dragged Curtis down the stairs in loud thuds and threw him on the ground close to Maura.

"You will be a more powerful warrior than ten armies." Buford patted her head. "Won't you, my little dog?"

Buford intended to turn her. He would be her master for all eternity.

"And then," Buford continued, "you'll introduce me to the others. We'll give them an invitation they cannot refuse. I will have a clan of MacGregor warlocks at my disposal."

Bloodlust would compel her to obey, and she would be a mindless creature who performed his bidding even if that meant leading him straight to her family.

"What about him?" Virgile kicked Curtis in the ribs.

"This rotted piece of flesh will be your first kill." Buford took much delight in the exposition of his plans for her, feeding off her fear of what was to come.

"No." Maura shook her head. Tears spilled at the thought of hurting Curtis or her family. She should have killed Buford when she had the chance. Now they were all dead anyway.

Buford's hand tightened in her hair, and he jerked her head back. Fangs bit into her neck. There was nothing gentle or seductive about the vampire's touch. She felt him draining the life from her, slurping and gnawing at her throat. Her use of magick had killed too much of their surroundings. Even if she had the energy to pull more power, there was nothing left to take.

Buford released his mouth and turned to bite his wrist. Blood ran down her shoulder from her neck. He pressed his wound against her lips to force his blood into her mouth.

"Maura!" Curtis sounded far away. She felt him grabbing for her. His hand slipped in her blood as blackness took hold.

Chapter Eight

"No. No, no, no, no…" Curtis gathered Maura's limp body in his arms. "Help me! Someone help!"

He didn't know how, but when he touched her bloody arm, they'd transported back to the MacGregor front hall. The trees were gone as if they'd never broke through the floor. Crimson smeared the white surface as he hooked an arm around her neck to lift her head.

Maura's anemic features didn't move. He swiped at her mouth, trying to remove any trace of Buford's blood from her lips before she had time to swallow.

Curtis felt the curse of the dhampir as blood soaked into his skin. It tingled, feeding the sleeping monster inside. He didn't care. He couldn't let Maura turn.

"MacGregors!" Curtis screamed. His heart hammered in fear.

"Aye, what's—" Rory appeared in the dining room entryway. Curtis has met Maura's brother at the Crimson Tavern. He'd married one of his waitresses. "Ma, we need ya! It's Maura! She's hurt!"

Iain and Euann ran in from the dining room. All three men rushed to Maura's side.

"What happened?" Rory demanded, pushing Curtis from his sister. "What did ya do?"

"Vampire." Curtis refused to back away as he took hold of Maura's hand. "Come on, Maura. Open your eyes, baby."

"Vampire?" Rory and Euann said in unison.

"Since when are there vampires in Green Vallis?" Iain demanded.

Their eyes turned accusing. Of course. It would be the dhampir's fault.

And maybe it was.

Curtis was the reason Virgile came to town. It was his connection to Buford that brought them to that point in the past. If he'd never have come to Green Vallis, Maura would not have been in danger.

But how could he have known all that?

"What's all the—*Maura*!" Cait ran across the

balcony above the front hall and rushed down the stairs, her heels clicking in hard strikes.

Curtis released Maura's hand as her mother charged forward. He crawled back on the floor out of her way. The blood on his hands caused him to slip on the marble.

"Who dared do this to my baby?" Cait demanded.

"Vampire," Rory said.

"We went back," Curtis tried to explain, but somehow the facts didn't seem necessary. Tears filled his eyes. How it happened didn't change what happened. "She… Please, can you save her?"

Cait put her hands on Maura's face then chest. She leaned close to the wound on her neck and touched the blood smearing her daughter's cheek. She rubbed it between her fingers.

"Rory, my kit," Cait ordered, taking charge of the situation. "Iain, find your wife. Tell her I'll need all the yarrow, calendula, and goldenrod she can get for me. Euann, alert the family. Vampires have declared war. Everyone is to be on high alert. No one goes anywhere alone."

The three men went to do as she ordered.

"Is she…?" Curtis could barely get the words past the feeling of his heart stuck in his throat. "Please save her. I can't lose…"

"The blood around her mouth feels like the blood I detected on your hand last night," Cait said. "Where did ya get it?"

He lifted his hand, taking a moment to remember. "That came from a wine bottle of blood we found in the mail carrier's pack."

"It had been tainted with dark magick. I'm guessing someone took the vampire's blood, did something to it, and then gave it back to him as some kind of spell. For what purpose, I don't know. I'd need a sample."

Cait continued to examine her daughter.

Curtis desperately wanted to help. "Maura mentioned recognizing an emblem for wizards who practiced dark magick in the 1800s on that letter we gave ya."

"The vampire who did this… It's the same blood ya have inside ya, isn't it?" Cait stroked the hair off Maura's forehead before pulling her eyelids open. "Stay with me, daughter. Stay with me."

Curtis felt no need to hide the family's shame after all that happened. "His name is Buford. He's my great grandfather."

Cait frowned and shook her head while still examining Maura. "The virus is trying to take hold, but you're fighting it, aren't ya, my brave daughter."

"Please…" he begged, knowing it wouldn't make a difference.

Cait glanced at him.

"Maybe you can petrify her. Stop the progress," Curtis suggested.

Cait looked at him like he was an idiot for thinking that would work. "Her magick is burnt out. I don't know how long she can continue to resist."

"We have to do something." Curtis leaned over to kiss Maura's forehead. She felt cool to the touch, and a lack of blood paled her skin.

"Do ya care for my daughter?"

Curtis nodded. "I feel like I've known her all my life. I can't imagine not knowing her."

"Will ya do anything to help her?" she insisted.

"Yes. Yes." He nodded. "Anything."

"Will ya give your life?" she asked.

Curtis nodded. "Yes. I'd give my life for her. Just, please, help her."

"I'm glad to hear that." Cait eyed him. "Because ya might be carrying the only thing in this entire world that can save her. But I'm not going to lie. It's going to hurt like hell, and you're going to wish ya were dead."

"I don't care," Curtis answered. "Do it. Whatever it is, do it."

"Got it," Rory appeared with a large bag.

"Find Margareta," Cait ordered her son, taking the bag. "Tell her to bring her knives, the special ones, and then fetch me all the towels ya can find. Then call Bruce and your father. Get them here."

Rory ran to do as he was told.

"Carry her." Cait strode into the dining room, not waiting to see if Curtis obeyed.

Curtis scooped Maura into his arms and hurried after the commanding woman, glad that someone seemed to have a plan.

The feel of blood against his skin turned from tingling to itching. Next would come uncontrollable rage. They strode through the dining room and kitchen before finally turning into the hall to go into Maura's room. Cait waved her hand, opening the door without touching it. The coffee cup was still on the floor. The woman kicked it out of the way as she walked past.

"In the tub." Cait pointed toward the bathroom door, opening it with her magick.

Curtis obeyed. He placed Maura in the tub and stepped back. Cait blocked his escape when he tried to move out of her way.

She wielded a knife. "Get in there with her."

Curtis did as she said. "I have to warn you. I

have a bad reaction to other people's blood on my skin."

"I know, dhampir, but trust me. In a little bit, that's not going to matter."

He opened his mouth to ask what she would do, but Cait waved her hand and took away his voice. He tried to reach for his throat, but his body wouldn't respond. He looked around but couldn't blink.

"Sorry, lad. Combatting vampire magick is ugly work. All dark magick comes with a steep price." Cait whispered, looming toward him with the blade. "This is about to get messy."

Chapter Nine

A river of blood and darkness that contained all the knowledge of human suffering held Maura in its depths. Every secret human pain churned in the crimson water. She screamed, trying to keep from going under, but her arms were tired, so tired. She attempted to use her magick, but there was only death, and she couldn't find the fuel she needed.

Maura awoke from the agony of her nightmares to an even more troubling scene— Raibeart's clown-painted face pressing close to hers. He grinned. She screamed, startled as she flailed her arms to get away from him. The bed she was on didn't allow for an easy escape.

"It's about time your lazy arse got up." Raibeart stood next to the bed. He wore oversized pants with red polka dots that ballooned at the thighs, thick yellow suspenders, and the kind of orange, curly clown wig only a haunted carnival could love.

Maura struggled to sit. She was in her bedroom at the MacGregor mansion. Her head throbbed in protest of the movement, but anything was better than swimming in Nightmare River.

"What in the name of all that is holy are ya wearing?" Maura's voice was hoarse, and she coughed at the effort it took to speak.

Raibeart's painted smile couldn't hide his grimace. "My sweet Abigail likes clowns. Make sure ya remember that."

She leaned back as he pointed a puffy gloved finger in her direction.

"She's a newborn. I'm not sure she likes anything beyond eating and pooping." Maura rubbed her eyes.

"Shows what ya know." Raibeart waddled toward the bedroom door. A light horn blast sounded with each step. "I'd rethink your attitude, or I won't let ya babysit."

"Let me…?"

Raibeart pulled open the door. "Your boyfriend's back from sunbathing."

"Boyfriend?" Maura leaned to see who was at

the door. Curtis stood in the doorway with his hand outstretched for the doorknob that moved out of his grasp. Dark circles marred the skin under his eyes, and he'd lost weight. He wore a kilt and white t-shirt but no shoes. A silver bracelet wrapped around his forearm.

"What would ya call him? Stalker? He's been glued to your side for three weeks, four if ya count the week he was unconscious next to ya. I don't." Raibeart waddled his giant pants out of Curtis's way. "Don't be looking at me like I'm your next snack. It's Rory's turn to feed ya."

"Maura? You're awake!" Curtis rushed past Raibeart to crawl next to her on the bed. His hands shook as he reached for her face. The second they touched, he sighed in relief. "You're warm."

"Probably because they have every blanket in the house stacked on this bed." She struggled to slide a leg free from its cushioned prison.

"Does Cait know she's awake?" Curtis asked Raibeart.

"I'm on my way to tell her now. By the way, Maura, I stashed a bottle of the good stuff under the bed. Looks like ya could use it. Don't let Cait see it." Raibeart waddled and honked his way from the room, leaving the door open behind him.

Maura caressed Curtis's cheek with the back

of her hand. A silver bracelet had been clasped on her wrist. "I have so many questions. I don't know where to begin."

Curtis glanced toward the door. "I think we all have questions where your uncle is concerned. I think it's safe to say which one in the family is the Loki."

"Sadly, that's all MacGregor. How long has he been in the clown suit?"

"About a week, I think. Before that, it was Captain Blueberry, a purple superhero with a cape. Your Aunt Margareta kept yelling at him for jumping off the top balcony to make Jewel giggle. And by purple, I mean he and Jewel were both stained head-to-toe purple."

Maura chuckled. The MacGregor normality of that statement comforted her somehow. "That sounds about right."

"I will give him one thing. For all his strangeness, he's been amazing with Abigail. I would not have fared half as well on my own." Curtis sighed and ran his thumb over her bottom lip. "I'm happy to see your eyes open. When I saw you on the ground, your mouth covered with… Well, you had us all very worried. How do you feel?"

"Hungover, maybe?" She ran her hands through her hair to feel the tangled mess. "And like I should probably find a mirror."

"You're beautiful," he assured her.

"If you're lying, I don't want to know." Maura tugged the thick stack of blankets off her legs and tried to throw them to the end of the bed. They were too heavy, so Curtis leaned over to help her. The familiar smell of her body wash emanated from his skin. His naked thigh poked out from the bottom hem of the kilt. She had to admit that she always enjoyed a man in a kilt. That article of clothing was one thing the Scots had definitely gotten right.

"Ya look exhausted." She touched his face as he had hers, running her thumb along the firm texture of his lips.

"I'm doing better. Cait is making me lay in direct sunlight out in the back gardens for fifteen minutes twice a day." He touched the kilt when her gaze went back to it. "She tried to get me to wear a speedo so the sun could hit more of my skin. We compromised on the kilt. After the miracle I saw her work with you, I'll do anything your ma tells me to."

"Careful, if she hears ya say that she'll start planning our wedding." Maura laughed.

"If that's a proposal, I'm not saying no." Curtis grinned.

"You're a very go-with-the-flow kind of guy, aren't ya?" Maura glanced at the empty doorway, wondering how much time they had before someone came to check on them.

"Mawmaw always says to trust your heart, follow your head, and know that both are fools more often than not. Always seemed like sound advice." He smiled. "We have technically been dating for a month now, and we've shared blood transfusions. Some would say that's pretty intimate."

"Was I really out for four weeks?" Maura tried to remember her nightmare in the river of pain. What felt never-ending at the time had now started to fade as dreams typically do.

Curtis nodded. "You're really into me, just so you know. You don't talk much, but I like a woman who knows how to listen. Plus, your family likes me."

She laughed, hitting his chest. "Be serious for a moment. What happened?"

"Buford bit you and then gave you his blood." His expression fell, and he touched her neck where the bite had been. "By all rights, you should be undead."

"That part I remember." Maura placed her hand over his, threading her fingers between his to feel if there was a scar. The skin had healed. "It's hard to forget."

"Somehow, we were brought back to the front

hall like last time. You almost turned." Curtis held her hand. "Your ma and aunt thankfully knew of a cure for the virus since it hadn't yet taken over your body."

"Silver?" Maura lifted the bracelet.

He showed her his matching jewelry. "They're binding bracelets to keep us from slipping back in time again. For the cure, they used dhampir blood."

"Your blood?" She studied his face, wondering if that is why he looked so worn. "Just how much did they take from ya?"

"It doesn't matter. They needed it because it came from the same vampire line as the one who attacked you. And it worked." Curtis looked as if he would say more but instead glanced at the open door.

Maura automatically lifted her hand to give them privacy. Her magick was weak, and the door creaked and swayed.

Curtis stood, going to push it closed quietly. When he returned, he stood by the bed. "I need to tell you that I told your family elders everything. I hope that was the right thing to do. At the time, I was worried that leaving out any detail would risk your life. Cait knew you had burned out your magick and wanted to know how." He stepped closer. "But I've had time to think about it, and

I've worried that maybe you wouldn't want anyone to know about what happened to the vampire army. It wasn't my secret to tell, and I'm sorry."

"It's all right. I'm not proud of it, but…" A tear slipped over Maura's cheek. "That drummer boy. He was so young."

"And he was already dead." Curtis wrapped his arms around her and held her close. "They all were. The virus had taken root inside of them, and their souls were already cursed to march for all eternity. Think of how many lives you saved by stopping fifty-plus vampires from feeding. There isn't enough blood in the United States to sustain that many feeders. They'd kill off half of the population within a generation."

"I'm sorry." She swiped another tear. "I know I should have killed Buford and Virgile, too. Maybe I could have stopped all of this. But then you'd be dead too, back then, and I don't know what that would have meant when I returned without ya. I couldn't… I didn't want…"

Maura searched his face, unable to find the words to express what she felt. So, instead, she kissed him.

From that first moment, there had been something between them, that soft energy, a connection that ran like an undercurrent to her magick. Now that her powers were weakened, she felt their link stronger than before. She imagined she felt his blood inside her, moving through her veins, joining them even more.

Maura pulled at his t-shirt, wanting to feel his skin against her. As his arms raised, she broke their kiss to lift the shirt over his head. Her eyes went to his muscled chest as she leaned in to kiss him there.

Long marks gouged his flesh, the edges red as if they had not had much time to heal. She gasped, pulling back to look at what had been done.

"Maura?" His voice was muffled, and she realized she gripped the shirt halfway off him, covering his face and trapping his arms. She let go.

Curtis jerked the shirt over his head and tossed it aside.

Maura lightly touched the edge of one of the wounds. "My family did this to ya?"

"It looks worse than it is," he assured her.

"I don't see how." Maura pulled his arm to look at his sides and back. He turned to let her see. The same scars had been dug into his back. Tears stung her eyes as she realized just how much pain he'd gone through to save her. "My ma shouldn't have done this."

Curtis turned in a full circle and then crawled up on the bed next to her. He cupped her face and kissed the tears from her cheeks. "Yes, she should have. I told her to."

"No." Maura shook her head.

"The vampiric curse is one of the darkest. Margareta said that to fight such darkness, sacrifices had to be made. It was a small thing to ask to save your life. I would go through it a thousand times if I had to."

No person had ever done so much for her.

Maura knew her aunt was right. Magick didn't just appear out of nowhere. They were lucky that most times they could take from nature, hurting only trees and plants. But to stop someone from turning into a vampire?

"Thank ya for saving me." Maura kissed him softly before pulling back.

She found herself mesmerized by his eyes as he gazed into hers. Everything about this man spoke to her on a primal level. She focused on the sound of his breathing, enjoying the fact that they were both alive and together. His body called to hers like a magnet, pulling her closer with that invisible force. Their shared passion fueled her, and her head began to clear.

The bedroom door began to open. Maura lifted her hand and slammed it shut before forcing the lock to latch. She was tired of being interrupted every time they kissed.

She didn't ask who it was. "Come back later!"

Curtis chuckled. "It seems your magick is getting stronger."

"I guess I just needed the right fuel." She pulled out of her t-shirt and threw it aside. Since she wasn't wearing a bra, she was able to close the distance between their flesh. Her breasts pressed into him, and she inhaled sharply at the contact. "Ya did offer to refuel me."

"Did I?" He ran his hand up and down her naked back.

"On our first date when we were in the field," she reminded him, kissing his neck. "Remember?"

"Of course, and I'm happy to oblige. Anything for you, Maura." Curtis laid her back on the bed gently, as if she were the most fragile thing in the world. He lay next to her, careful to keep his weight shifted to the side.

Magick stirred and grew, awakened by the soft press of his mouth and the stroke of his hands. His lips adored every inch they could reach, trailing over her cheek and neck.

Maura felt his arousal against her thigh and urged her pajama pants to dissolve from her body. She pushed up his kilt with her naked leg. Even though this was their first time coming together, he was familiar to her, as if their feelings were beyond time and space, beyond a single moment. She felt as if they had loved each other for a thousand lifetimes, and in a thousand different ways, only their timelines were like pieces of a giant puzzle that needed to be put back together in the proper order. This was their first kiss, their twentieth, their last.

In a world that did not make sense, Curtis was the only logic she needed.

And she loved him.

She had heard that true love was like this, a rush of feeling and realizations. Her magick had been trying to tell her, but she hadn't been listening. After centuries of living, she would have remembered feeling this way with someone else. There was no one else. Only Curtis.

The warm probe of his tongue traced her lips. Her body tingled where they touched and ached where they didn't. This had to be what perfection felt like.

"Curtis," she whispered his name, wanting him to soothe the need deep inside of her.

Her magick called to him, heightening their already rampant desires. She drew her hands over his hips, pulling him on top of her to settle between her legs. Her fingers ran along his fresh scars, and it reminded her of how much he'd sacrificed to save her life. She explored his body, squeezing his flexing ass to draw him into her.

He pressed his hips forward. The brush of his arousal left her both euphoric and breathless. Her body began to glow, her magick snaking out of her body to envelop him in her pleasure.

His mouth opened as he lifted above her, but no words were needed as he thrust deep. Pleasure built between them. They came together, rocking with increasing speed as perfection erupted into chaos. Her heart pounded so loudly in her ears she was sure the entire world could hear it.

And then it happened, the beautiful madness of release. She inhaled sharply, letting the intense climax roll through her. Curtis tensed, as elated at the moment as she. Nothing mattered beyond these feelings.

His head dropped forward to press against hers. Their breath mingled as her magick glow faded back into her skin.

Curtis moved to lay next to her, careful to keep his weight off her. He was always so considerate and protective of her. He made her feel safe.

"Hey," she whispered.

Curtis kissed her temple.

"Would ya check under the bed for the good stuff?" she asked.

He chuckled but rolled off the bed. Curtis

disappeared beneath the side of the bed, and she heard him fumbling around. When he reappeared, it was with a bottle of Scotch with only about a quarter of the contents left.

"Ooh, good year," Maura said. Curtis opened it and then offered her a drink. She took a long gulp and coughed at the burn it caused. She went to take another drink.

"I've wanted to ask," Curtis said. "Who's Rodney?"

Maura spat the drink out in surprise. "Why on earth are ya asking about him?"

"Euann and Iain mentioned something. Actually, they said it like a warning."

Maura laughed and handed him the bottle. "He was a doorman in New York who had a slight crush on me. I didn't return his feelings, so to get my attention he…"

"What?" Curtis held the bottle, ready to drink.

"He made a giant butter sculpture depicting our wedding." Maura scrunched up her face. "I have not been able to live it down. My cousins like to tease me with that poor Rodney bit."

"That's a relief. I was worried I had some competition." Curtis chuckled and finished the bottle. Then, looking at the empty bottle, he shrugged and rolled it back under the bed.

"Not if ya know how to sculpt with a root

vegetable. It's pretty hard to beat butter." Maura patted the blanket for him to return to his place next to her.

"I've been told my tater tots are life changing." He resumed his place next to her. "Next time you're at the tavern, I'll arrange them into the shape of a happy face."

She laughed. "Be still my heart!"

Maura couldn't stop smiling. The liquor burned, and she hoped that this time when she dreamed it wouldn't be of nightmares. She snuggled into Curtis's arms, knowing there was so much she needed to think about and unable to remember what any of it was.

Chapter Ten

For the first time in a long time, vivid nightmares did not disrupt Maura's sleep. There were no bloody battles, no rivers filled with a painful death. Instead, she felt like she floated through an endless forest where the magick never ran dry. Her body split into hundreds of pieces, each drifting without aim.

"Hey."

That one word caused all her pieces to crash to the forest floor.

"Hey."

Something hard poked her arm. She gasped, opening her eyes to the reality of the MacGregor mansion bedroom.

"Hey, sis, how ya feeling? Remember, I'm your

favorite brother, so if you're craving a snack, eat Rory." Bruce stood over her. Bright yellow paint smudged his cheek. She stared at it in confusion.

"Uh…?" Maura tried to speak. She looked at the bed, but Curtis was gone. Thankfully, her magick had helped dress her in a nightgown before she fell asleep.

"Shh, don't try to talk." Bruce patted her arm. "Ma said we're not supposed to overtire ya. So, listen, I have some good news. I changed the name of the motel since ya hated it. We're now called the Canary Cage. Each guest suite has a disaster history theme to enlighten and teach, and no one is naked. Well, only one painting is naked, but it was the sex candle wax incident of 2002 so really naked makes sense."

"Canary…?" Maura frowned.

"Clever, right? Canary Cage." Bruce grinned. "Like when they took birds down into the mines because they were sensitive to gases and one dying would be a warning that a mining disaster was coming."

"What…no." Maura shook her head and tried to sit up. "Bruce, ya can't—"

"I took care of it. I even forged your signature on all the paperwork, so ya don't have to worry about a thing." Bruce backed his way to the door. "I'll tell ma you're awake. I'm happy you're alive."

Maura tugged the thick covers off her legs, but he was gone before her feet touched the floor. She swayed and held onto the bed. It had been a long while since she'd been upright.

"Please tell me you're joking," Maura said to the empty room. She'd forgotten all about the motel and the fact that Bruce would have been left in charge during her absence. There was no telling what he'd done to the place.

Canary Cage?

Maura had no room in her brain to process Bruce's latest idea. All she could think was, thank goodness her family didn't require the money.

Maura needlessly reached her hand across the empty bed, wishing Curtis would appear. She wondered if he bathed in the sunlight as ordered by her ma.

Under normal circumstances, Maura didn't waste magick on the simple tasks of the day—like getting dressed and combing her hair—but this morning, she made an exception. As she stepped toward the bedroom door, her nightgown fell behind her to be replaced by jeans and blue top. Comfortable shoes appeared on her feet, and she felt her hair pulling around her head as it righted itself.

Maura paused in the doorway, taking several deep breaths as she waited for the dizziness to subside. The soft murmur of voices came from the direction of the dining room, and she gravitated toward the noise.

"There's no need to fret over the small things, ya did well, my Cait. Our girl is alive." Her father's voice held a steady calm. Many people thought Cait was the rational one in her marriage because she was so put together, but Murdoch was the glue that kept her grounded. His easygoing nature complemented Cait's high stress levels.

"Ya both did well," Uncle Angus added, presumably to include her Aunt Margareta in the compliment. "That was a real feat of magick."

"I don't know. Would it be so bad if she turned? I think having a vampire in the family could be kind of cool. We could open a whole new blood bank market." Rory's comment was met with the sound of two steady smacks. "Ow —ow! I was joking. Joking!"

"Curtis is half vampire," Euann mused. "He's a pretty solid guy. He gave us family discounts on tater tot nachos."

"I agree. Maura should marry that one," Rory added. "I call for an official family vote that Maura be forced to make Curtis a MacGregor."

"Anyway, as I was saying," Kenneth interrupted in his all-business tone, ignoring Rory's nonsense. "Erik called. Lydia sold out of all her bath products at the convention, and they have three major distribution offers for Love Potions on the table. He's sending them over for the lawyers to look over."

Even though her cousin Erik had his own MacGregor responsibilities, he more often than not was busy helping his wife build her lotion empire, Love Potions.

"Fergus and Donna checked in from Europe," Kenneth continued. With Jewel needing constant parental supervision, his main job was to act as the family business coordinator. He kept track of all of them. "They have concerns about that food chain's hiring practices and have passed on the acquisition. They're now on their way to vacation at Easter Island. Malina and Dar are back in Vegas. Niall and Charlotte haven't checked in, but they're not meant to for another week, as Niall is tracking a waheela reported to be in the Canadian wilderness. Oh, and Euann, your friend Mrs. Callister has started yet another blog. Presumably, we might be the CIA."

"On it," Euann answered. "Her new site will crash harder than Cinderella's carriage after the royal ball."

"Whatever that means," Kenneth said. "And that's all the updates I have."

"Great! Is this family meeting over? I promised

Jane I'd help her at the community garden." Iain appeared through the kitchen doorway as he stood from the table. "Maura, it's good to see ya up and around."

Maura lifted her hand in acknowledgment as she walked into the dining room. Her family was around the table. Her parents, Margareta, and Angus sat at one end with her cousins and Rory at the other, except for Iain, who ducked away to help his wife.

"Am I missing a family meeting?" Maura asked, wishing they'd all stop looking at her like she was a party-crashing zombie.

"Don't worry about it," Margareta said. "Bruce can take care of the motel. Business should be the last thing on your mind."

"Maura." Her mother came at her, arms outstretched. "Don't ya ever scare me like that again!"

Maura braced herself for the hard hug that lasted way too long. Her father wrapped his arms around both women, keeping the embrace going longer.

"Maura, lassie," was all Murdoch said, but his love radiated from those brief words.

"Let the poor thing go," Margareta ordered. "Ya will sap her strength."

Margareta patted Maura's shoulder as her parents released her. "Sit down. I'll bring ya food. Cait, give me a hand."

Maura took a seat next to Angus. "Which one is the waheela again? The snow beast?"

"Giant wolfs with a penchant for beheading people," Angus answered as he lovingly squeezed her around the shoulders. "You're thinking of Old Yellow Top. He's Big Foot's cousin."

"Right." Maura nodded.

"Kenneth, your turn," Margareta yelled from the kitchen.

Kenneth sighed. He started to roll up his sleeve as he walked toward the kitchen.

"Dish duty?" Maura asked with a small laugh.

"Bloodletting," Rory answered. He lifted his arm from beneath the table to show a bandage. Euann pulled up his long t-shirt to show the same. "Someone's got to feed your new boyfriend."

Maura started to answer but didn't know what to say.

"Rory, stop tormenting your sister. He doesn't eat it," Murdoch stated. "It's for a salve. The ceremony to save your life nearly killed him. If he'd been human, he would never have survived it. Your ma is slowly reintroducing blood into his system."

"If he needs blood, I'll give him mine," Maura said. "We can do a transfusion."

"He's a dhampir," her da stated.

"So?" Maura frowned.

"It means I have a kind of allergic reaction to other people's blood," Curtis stated from the doorway. He nodded at the table in general. "Hey, guys."

"Anaphylaxis?" She tried to stand, but he motioned for her to stay as he came to sit beside her.

"More like an abominable snowman on crystal meth." Curtis leaned to kiss her cheek. "Minus the body hair."

Euann began to snicker.

"What?" Rory asked.

"I just thought of a period joke," Euann laughed harder.

"Keep that one to yourself," Maura ordered.

"I'm, uh, going to go help…" Angus stood. "Murdoch?"

"Aye," Murdoch answered.

Both elders disappeared into the kitchen.

Maura slipped her hand onto Curtis's naked knee under the table as she leaned toward him. He looked healthier. The dark circles were no longer under his eyes. "How are ya feeling?"

"Better now that you're awake." He held her hand.

"Euann, I'm taking your car!" Raibeart yelled from the front hall.

"What?" Euann shot up in his seat and ran after him. "No! Raibeart, stop!"

Rory laughed. "Euann just found where Raibeart left the corvette last time he stole it."

"Where was it?" Curtis asked.

"He'd parked it in the forest stream." Rory's attention turned to the window. They watched as Euann ran down the driveway chasing his car. "So, uh, Curtis, now that Maura is cured and all, any chance you'll be reopening the kitchen at Crimson Tavern?"

"Rory, come on!" Maura frowned at her brother.

"People need to eat, Maura," Rory countered.

"Aye, they do." Margareta carried a tray from the kitchen and set it down on the table. "We have all your favorites." She began taking plates from the tray and set them in front of Maura. "Mac and cheese. Mashed potatoes. Lemon cake. Fried Chicken. Donuts. Popcorn. Sliced tomato and fresh mozzarella."

Her ma appeared with a second tray and began taking over service. "Beef stroganoff. Baked potato. Sesame chicken. Hamburger. Waffle fries. Brownie."

Rory started to reach for the burger. "I'll take that hamburger if ya don't want—"

Cait slapped her son's hand. "Your sister is recovering."

"So am I," Rory protested.

"From?" Cait put her hands on her hips.

"Having Maura as a sister," Rory answered.

Cait threw up her hands and left.

Kenneth came from the kitchen, rolling down his sleeve over a bandaged arm. "Curtis, I'm supposed to send ya into the lion's den."

Curtis patted Maura's hand and stood. "I'll be back."

Raibeart strode past the window, his kilt covered in mud. Seeing their attention on him, he smiled and gave a jaunty wave before coming into the house. Stopping at the doorway, he grinned. "He'll never find it this time. I hid it well."

"That was fast," Rory answered.

"Aye. Next time he'll think twice before messing with my favorite golf clubs," Raibeart answered.

"Where are the girls?" Kenneth asked.

"Calm down, laddie. They're with Andrea getting their baths," Raibeart dismissed.

Kenneth left, and his footsteps could be heard on the stairs.

Raibeart pointed at the table and then wiggled his fingers. A spoon flipped over into the bowl of mashed potatoes. He gestured again, and the bowl floated toward him. He snatched it out of the air.

Maura grabbed the burger and locked eyes with Rory as she took a big bite. "Mm, so good."

"I liked ya better when ya were in a coma," Rory mumbled.

She knew it wasn't true. Joking was their way of showing affection for each other.

Maura took another bite and then handed it to him. "Don't tell ma."

"Wouldn't dream of it. She might get the impression we like each other." Rory grinned and carried the burger out of the dining room to avoid getting caught with it.

Maura turned her attention to the waffle fries. She grabbed a handful before going to check what was happening to Curtis.

Aunt Margareta and her ma had Curtis's arms trapped over his head with his shirt as they drew lines of red salve down his scars from two bowls. They whispered an incantation. The scars visibly shifted, closing a little more as they healed.

"That's odd," Cait said, sniffing the bowl. "I

wonder if we got the ingredients right. They've never healed much before."

Margareta looked at Maura and then Curtis. "It's almost like he got a big dose of magick." She winked at her niece.

"No." Cait shook her head. "I'm sure I used the same amount."

Curtis pulled down his shirt. "Thank you, ma'ams."

"Ya should be eating." Cait pointed at her daughter, shooing her from the room. "We have this under control."

Maura held up the handful of fries. "I am eating."

"Would ya like to check on Abigail with me?" he asked.

Maura nodded.

When they walked through the dining room, he snagged a donut from the table. Maura took more fries. She loved her family but was grateful when they didn't try to follow them.

"They're a lot to take in, I know," she said.

"They have a good energy," Curtis replied diplomatically. "And they took in me and my grandmother. They saved you. I'll be forever indebted."

Maura lifted the back of his shirt to check the scars. "They're looking good, considering."

Curtis ate the donut in a couple of bites.

"So what do ya think happens now?" Maura asked as they went up the marble staircase. She stepped over clumps of mud that had fallen from Raibeart's kilt.

"I'm not sure. I haven't told mawmaw about baby mawmaw, but I did call and check on her. She's alive. Sounded like her normal self. I think at some point we'd have to get the baby back to her own time with her own people." Curtis guided Maura's lower back with his hand as they neared the top. "Before she's old enough to remember being here."

Maura nodded in agreement. "We don't want to risk altering the past any more than we have."

Doors leading to bedrooms lined the wall opposite the balcony. They turned down a hallway and headed into the east wing.

"If we did alter history, how would we know? Would we remember when we got back if it had changed? You could have previously loved white gloves and had, I don't know, pink hair."

"That's a headache-inducing thought." Maura shook her head. "Though, I can tell ya for a fact I never liked white gloves. That was true before the 1800s."

A child's laughter came from one of the bedrooms, and pink glitter exploded through an opened door. Jewel's room was the thing of every little girl's dreams. Literally. The child had the power to affect her environment, even with the binding bracelets her stepmother kept on her. Andrea had been destined to care for Jewel. The pair were bonded as close as any blood relations.

Crystal star prisms hung from the ceiling, causing rainbowed light to dance on the walls. A blue princess bed with ruffles sat in the middle of a ball pit moat. Rory's dog, a schipperke named Jim slept on the bed in a sparkly dress. A pile of stuffed animals littered the floor, and Maura knew that Jewel often jumped over the ball pit from her bed onto them to cushion her landing.

"Rawr!" Jewel jumped from behind a stuffed bear and curled her fingers into claws. She wore bear pajamas complete with a hood.

"Don't worry." Andrea appeared from the bathroom. "She's wearing the binding bracelet. No real claws this time."

Maura laughed and showed Jewel her arm. "Us too, kid."

Jewel giggled, seeming pleased that someone else had the bracelet too.

"Where's Abigail?" Curtis asked.

Jewel got on her hands and knees, crawling dramatically like a bear. "Rawr. Rawr. Rawr…"

With each step, her roars became softer. Jewel

led them to the baby bouncer near the stuffed animal pile. Abigail slept in a teddy bear outfit that matched Jewel's.

"Abby," Jewel announced before leaning to kiss the baby's forehead. "Shh. Quiet."

"Where are my bear cubs?" Raibeart appeared in a bear costume and began to dance his way into the room.

"Oh, wow." Curtis drawled under his breath. "That's…something."

"At least it's not as creepy as the clown," Maura whispered.

Curtis nodded in agreement.

"Come on, let's play bear cubs." Maura went to the pile of stuffed animals and sat down next to the sleeping baby.

"Rawr," Jewel told them.

"Rawr," Maura answered. "We're going to hibernate with Abby."

Curtis sat down on the other side of the bouncer. He lightly touched Abigail's cheek. "She is pretty adorable, isn't she? And to think, she'll grow up to be the kind of woman that takes in a moody, grieving teenager no one else wanted. She saved my life."

"And ya saved hers." Maura pulled a giant stuffed bear next to her and rested against it. "There is something very beautiful about the symmetry of that."

"Hand me one of those bears." Curtis held out his hand and nodded toward the pile.

Maura laughed, tossing a fluffy pink one in his direction.

Chapter Eleven

The simple pleasure of watching a child play had been the most relaxing day Curtis had experienced in a long time. Jewel's happiness and innocence couldn't have contrasted his life more, and Abigail's soft suckling noises and sighs as she slept reminded him that time was a precious commodity.

When he looked at Maura, watching her smile, he knew she was the life he wanted. The MacGregor home was a house of love—hijinks, yes, but also love.

Curtis also knew that this was a life he might lose. He didn't express the fear to Maura, but he'd had a lot of time to think about their situation while she was mending. The only way he could think of to keep Abigail safe was to kill Buford and Virgile in the past before they had a chance to hurt anyone else. But if he erased that part of his history, it would change the course of his life. No one in his family would be raised with the threat of that family tree hanging over them. He might not need to leave Mississippi for work.

He might never meet *her*.

Curtis stared at Maura across the family dining table. The MacGregors feasted like it was their last meal. The cousins had brought their wives. Rory brought Jennifer. Bruce brought a paperback shoved in his back pocket.

Jewel sat on the floor with Abigail in her bouncer. Though he couldn't hear what was said, it looked as if she told the baby an animated story.

This was the life.

"So, Curtis, ya in?" Rory asked.

"I'm sorry?" Curtis has not been listening.

"Superbowl party at the tavern," Euann said. "Big screen television."

Curtis nodded. "Sounds awesome."

"And ya got to try the putting green Jane put in for us," Rory invited. "I have some clubs ya can borrow if ya don't have your own."

"Sounds great," Curtis answered.

"Hey, guys, come on. Easy," Maura protested. "He's my boyfriend, not yours."

Curtis grinned. Boyfriend? He liked the sound of that.

"Sorry, Maura," Rory said. "But the truth is, we're much more interesting company. And we all know he's dating ya to get to us."

"And we're cuter," Euann added.

"Aye, and cuter," Rory agreed.

"Leave her alone," Jennifer swatted her husband's arm. "Though, uh, Curtis, you are going to cater the party, right? That's one waitressing job perk I miss."

He laughed. "I can teach y'all how to make the tater tot nachos if you want."

"Nope, not the same," Iain said.

Laughter resumed as the family started telling stories of Cait's cooking mishaps which rolled over into Raibeart's humorously failed attempts to propose marriage to perfect strangers—some of which had been to a couple of his now-nieces.

Maura wiped her eyes as they teared with laughter. "He actually hacked a romance author's internet group thinking the members would be romantically inclined enough to accept his pro—"

A loud screech came from the front lawn, cutting off her words. Maura's expression fell into one of fear. They knew that sound.

Curtis spun around in his seat to look out the window.

"What…?" Kenneth began. "Jewel, honey, did ya summons a dragon again?"

"It's not her, Ken," Maura answered. "Vampires."

"Get away from the windows," Murdoch ordered.

Raibeart ran to the children and swooped Abigail into his arms. "Stay close, Jewel. Remember what we practiced earlier. This is the code red game."

More screeches sounded. Murdoch waved his hand to shut the curtains. Curtis moved toward Maura.

"The house is protected," Euann said. "I renewed the spells myself last week."

As if to deny his statement, a loud crash sounded upstairs, followed by another screech.

"Ma, we need weapons," Maura said.

"Library!" Cait motioned for them to follow her.

"Go," Murdoch ordered, even as he ran in the opposite direction to the front hall. Angus, Iain, Euann, Rory, and Bruce joined him.

The rest of the family rushed through the kitchen. Cait led them toward the library over-looking the back gardens.

"They're on the balcony!" Bruce's yell carried

from the front hall. A loud crack sounded as wood splintered from the balcony. "Watch out!"

Cait rushed to a bookshelf behind one of the oversized leather chairs and gestured with both hands to magickally force the books to move aside. They flew onto the floor. Behind the case was an arsenal cache—pistols, potion bottles, daggers, wooden stakes, amulets. They all began talking at once, stunted conversations running into each other.

"In the corner," Raibeart ordered Jewel. He held Abigail as he went next to Jewel.

"What breed of vampire?" Cait asked them.

The screeches became deafening.

Maura shook her head at her mother. "I don't know. They can fly."

"Don't leave her," Margareta ordered Raibeart. She tossed the man a stake. "It's on ya to keep those babies safe."

"With my life," Raibeart agreed. Curtis had never seen the man so serious.

"Curtis?" Cait prompted. "Breed?"

"Code red!" Raibeart ordered, huddling to protect Jewel and Abigail. The girl cried, and a forcefield bubble appeared around the three of them. "Close your eyes, Jewel, don't look."

"We never talked about that stuff in my family," Curtis answered. "They shift into man-bats. Hideous ones, too, when they do. Buford sounds like he's from like Lithuania or something. I don't even know if that's his real name."

"Wooden stakes it is, then. Ya stabbed that one in the woods with a branch. We'll have to hope that works on these others," Cait said.

A transparent blue film covered the weapons. Cait moved her hand slowly through the barrier as if the act took considerable effort. She pulled out batches of stakes and handed them to Margareta to pass around.

Abigail cried. Maura's eyes met his. All the love in Curtis' heart was in this room. There was so much he wanted to say to her, but they had once again run out of time.

Margareta thrust a stake at him. "Use it well."

"Ma!" Rory appeared in the doorway, holding his bloody stomach. "It's da. They—"

Blood coughed from his mouth, and he gagged on the words. Rory dropped to his knees. Maura screamed. Cait charged the door wielding a stake. She stabbed a gangly-looking creature in the chest. The vampire screeched and retreated before the flames of his death lit from somewhere beyond the library. Sounds of chaos erupted anew as Margareta charged into battle.

Cait kneeled by her son. "Rory, no! Rory!"

Maura started to reach for her mother but then suddenly pivoted. "Raibeart, give us the baby."

"No!" Raibeart denied. "We can keep her safe."

The way Euann had explained it to him, Jewel could have the power to stop the vampire attack. However, none of them would want to traumatize the child. As a phoenix, her magick came with one very horrible catch. If she had to tap into a significant surge of power, the child would flame out to be reborn. She would be a different kid. Kenneth had already lost three daughters. Curtis would never ask to sacrifice a terrified, crying six-year-old to save himself.

"We have to go back." Maura tried to reach through the force field, but it was too strong.

Cait screamed in anger, cursing in a language he didn't understand. She ran toward the battle, arms raised and magick streaming.

The family's screams filtered in from the other room. Curtis stood in the doorway, torn between protecting Maura and wanting to join the fight.

"Please, it's the only way." Maura pleaded. She motioned at Rory's dead body. "We have to stop this before it starts."

She yanked the binding bracelet from her wrist.

"Aye. Ya got it this time, Maura." Raibeart kissed the baby on the head and handed her out of the bubble. Abigail still wore her bear costume.

Someone had dropped a stake on the floor. Curtis gathered the weapon.

"Curtis, take off your binding bracelet," Maura said, cradling Abigail against her chest.

Curtis pulled the jewelry down his arm and dropped it on the floor. Through the doorway, he saw a blood-covered Buford striding toward them. He wrapped his arms around Maura and Abigail. Magick shot from Jewel's bubble, but it did not affect the vampire as it bounced off him and exploded against the ceiling.

"Raibeart, we need that ghost army," Maura yelled.

Raibeart repeated the request, telling Jewel to bring the tree people back.

Drums sounded. Buford appeared, snarling in rage and covered in blood. The drummer boy materialized near the bookcase. Soldiers appeared on the dark lawn outside the window.

Curtis hurled both of his stakes at Buford like darts but a golden amulet the vampire wore acted like a force field repelling the missiles.

Curtis yanked Maura and the baby toward the

drummer boy. As soon as their bodies hit the icy figure, he felt time shift. The room disappeared into a darkened forest. The battle noise stopped, and all that remained was the crying of a scared newborn to break the silence.

Chapter Twelve

Maura handed Abigail to Curtis before dropping to her hands and knees. They had appeared in a small grove of dead trees. Brown leaves still clung to their lifeless branches. Maura knew they had gone back to after she'd vanquished the vampire army. Her magick had done this. It seemed fitting since she felt as drained as these trees inside.

Shock and grief filled every inch of Maura's being. Her body rocked back and forth. She gasped for breath, feeling as if she couldn't get enough air.

"I felt them go," Maura whispered, clutching her chest as tears rolled down her face. "He killed them. Curtis, I felt their magick...leave...me. I can't...breathe. Empty. So empty. I can't..."

Curtis joined her on the ground. The soft glow

of moonlight illuminated his face. Holding the baby with one arm, he wrapped the other around her shoulders. "It hasn't happened yet."

Maura felt the hollow growing inside her soul. No words could take the pain of losing her family away, but what he said gave her hope.

"There's time to change the future." Curtis kept her close, comforting her. "We kill Buford and Virgile. Here. Now."

"What if it doesn't work? What if when we go back it's already done, and time just keeps flowing from that moment?" Maura swiped at her face with shaking hands.

Curtis didn't have an answer.

Maura took a deep breath, steadying herself. Now was not the time to stop. She knew they had to try. Of course, they had to try.

If this worked, her family would be saved.

If this worked, she'd lose the man she loved.

They would return to a future where they probably would never meet. Without Buford looming over his family, who knew what his life would be? Would he even be the same man he was now? One way or the other, she'd suffer a horrendous loss. Maura clutched at his arm.

"Curtis. I need to tell ya…" Her voice caught as she looked at him. "I lov—"

"No," he stopped her. "You're going to tell me

when we find each other again in the future. And I'm going to tell you the same. I will not lose you, Maura. I can't believe there is any version of fate that doesn't have you in my life."

She nodded. "OK."

"OK," he repeated.

Abigail continued to fuss.

"What should we do with Abigail?" Maura asked. "Look for her ma?"

"Hazel died in childbirth," Curtis reminded her. "At least, that's what my mawmaw told me. I have to assume that part of history didn't change. Knowing it happened to my mother as well, I don't think my great grandmother could have survived a dhampir birth in any timeline, but especially not in the middle of a cabin without medical care."

"Did she ever talk about the people who took her in?"

"Not really," Curtis answered. "She called the man who raised her Papa and told me some funny stories about him. It's like I've said before. We didn't discuss the family shame, which often meant we didn't discuss the past at all. Most of what I know came from my dad. I was a teenager when he died and still had my head up my own ass. I never thought to ask questions about it."

Maura tried to focus on their surroundings,

feeling for hints of nature she could use. She slipped out of his embrace and stood to look at the trees. The forest wasn't in good condition. Many of the trees had died, and others were barely hanging on to life. "This is my fault. My magick decimated this forest."

"Nature will reclaim itself and heal in time," he said.

Grief still left her shaky, but she pushed through it, forcing herself to concentrate on the fight ahead. "OK. Let's figure this out. These are the trees by the plantation. It's night, so the vampires are flying around somewhere. They know—knew—Hazel in the slave quarters. Someone there probably, hopefully, took in her baby after she died."

"Ida and Joe," Curtis stated as if coming to a decision. He ambled to his feet and stared at Abigail as he bounced her lightly in his arms. "What do you think, mawmaw? Are they good people? Will they give you a good life?"

"I have a good sense about them." Maura stroked the baby's hair. "I could tell Ida cared for Hazel. She risked being out during the night under the threat of vampires to help a friend, a friend who was giving birth to Buford's baby."

Joe and Ida were also their only real option.

Curtis took a deep breath, nodding. "Which way to the cabins?"

"Reveal yourself," Maura said.

"Who's there?" Curtis asked, hunching over to shield the baby.

"Location spell," Maura answered, peering into the darkness for a hint of life. She detected blue lights through the trees and pointed toward them. "That way."

"I don't see anything," Curtis said.

"It wasn't your spell, so ya wouldn't be able to," Maura answered. "They're this way."

Curtis began shuffling his feet on the forest floor.

"What are ya doing?" she asked.

"We need weapons. I threw mine while we were escaping. Look for branches that we can use as stakes." Curtis swept his foot near the base of a couple of trees.

"It didn't work on Buford. He has some kind of amulet that protects him." Even so, Maura kneeled on the ground and began searching. Since Virgile had died that way before, he would probably die that way again.

"Here." Curtis slid a long, knobby branch toward her with his foot. "I got pretty close and personal with Buford when he flew us from this forest last time. He didn't have the amulet with him then. He must have gotten it after we escaped."

"That's probably the moment he became focused on finding my family." Maura grabbed both ends of the stick and pressed her foot into the middle, breaking it in two. She ran her hand over the tips, manifesting enough of her magick to sharpen them. She felt leaves trembling and falling from a distant sick tree to do it. "That'll do."

Maura carried the stakes as she led him through the woods, careful to muffle her steps the best she could. They came upon the back of the cabins and stopped within the trees.

Curtis searched the sky as Maura cautiously stepped forward. Not seeing any movement in the shadows, she waved her hand for him to follow. The baby fussed, and they both tensed and stopped walking. After several seconds, the baby quieted, and they continued toward Old Joe's home.

They stayed behind the cabins. The sound of horses came from a small stable. The young boy who'd taken their horse on their first visit came from within the structure. He glanced at them in surprise, staring as if trying to decide if they were friendly.

Maura held the stakes in her hands and automatically hid them from the kid's view behind her arms.

"Is Old Joe home?" Curtis asked.

The boy stared for a long while more before finally nodding. He gestured for them to follow before running ahead around the side of the cabin. By the time they made it to the front, Old Joe was standing on the porch. The boy watched from the doorway.

"I told you. It's the angel," the boy whispered. "She's the one who killed all the night feeders."

Joe frowned, waving the lad back. "And I told you to get inside. Get!"

The boy reluctantly obeyed, shutting the door. However, it remained open a crack, and she could see his eye peeking out at them.

Old Joe took his time studying them. Maura kept the stakes pressed behind her arms next to her body.

"Is that Hazel's baby?" Joe nodded toward Abigail.

Curtis nodded. "Yes, sir. It is."

"Did Hazel…?" Maura started to ask.

Joe shook his head before she could finish. "We buried her last week."

"Did she have other family?" Maura asked. "This child needs a home."

"Us. We're her family." Ida pushed open the door and stepped next to her husband.

"Ida," Joe began in protest.

"We're her family, Joseph Jefferson," Ida stated firmly.

Joe nodded, not naysaying his wife.

Maura and Curtis shared a look at the man's name.

Ida didn't meet Maura's gaze, but she looked over Curtis and Abigail. "Boy, what is that child wearin'?"

"Oh, uh." Curtis shrugged.

"Bear pajamas," Maura said.

Ida gave her a quick glance before holding out her arms to Curtis. "I'll take her. Night's no place for a baby around these parts. It's no place for the livin' either. You best get inside."

Curtis kissed Abigail on the head. "I'll be seeing you real soon, mawmaw."

Ida took the baby and began rocking it like an old pro. Maura wanted to touch Abigail and say goodbye, but the stakes hiding in her hands kept her from moving.

"Her name's Abigail. She's got a kind, good heart." Curtis looked as if he wanted to follow as Ida started to carry Abigail inside. "She likes clowns."

Ida gave him a strange look, arching her brow

but nodding. "It's all right, Abigail. Let's get you out of the dark." She nudged open the door with her foot. "Frank, run and fetch Maggie. This baby needs to be fed. Be quick."

The boy darted out of the house, leaping off the side of the porch as he sprinted down the road between the cabins.

"His name is Frank Jefferson?" Curtis asked.

"My son. Yes." Old Joe nodded.

Curtis smiled a little.

"Which way to the Big House from here?" Maura asked.

The man pointed. "You don't want to be goin' there. Hazel's cabin is empty if y'all want to stay there for the night."

"Thank you, but there's something we came here to do." Curtis reached to take one of the stakes from Maura.

Since their weapons were no longer a secret, Maura let her stake drop into a more comfortable position. "It's important that ya make sure everyone stays inside tonight. Don't let anyone follow us."

"Ma'am, no one's goin' outside this night or any night if they don't have to," Joe assured them.

"I hope that changes for you real soon." Curtis extended his hand.

Joe glanced at the weapons but then gave him a quick shake.

"Thank you, sir, for keeping Abigail safe," Curtis said.

When Old Joe retreated into the house, Curtis stared at the door.

Maura lightly touched his arm. "They have your last name. Jefferson. This is where she's supposed to be."

"I didn't think it would be this hard to leave her behind."

The boy appeared as if out of darkness, leaping onto the porch.

"Hey, Frank," Curtis said. "Nice to meet you. I'm Curtis."

Frank gave a shaky nod and didn't speak. He kept his back to the cabin's exterior wall as he sidestepped to the front door.

"We have to move." Maura tugged Curtis's arm. They had done what they needed to for Abigail. They delivered her to the right family. "What was that about with the kid?"

"My pawpaw's name was Frank." Curtis glanced back toward the cabin. "Mawmaw once told me she'd loved him her whole life."

Maura smiled. "This unquestionably is where Abigail belongs."

At least in this one task, they had done well. They protected the baby and got her home.

Maura's thoughts turned back to her family. Her smile fell as the emptiness washed through her anew. It would have been so easy to fall to the ground in grief and never get up. Her hand trembled as she lifted the stake to look at it. She tried to stop crying, but the tears spilled over.

"Hey." Curtis put his hand on her shoulder. "Stay with me, Maura. Focus on what we need to do."

"I can't shake the strangest feeling that we've been here before and that it's not going to end well," she said.

"Because we have more or less been here before. But it's not over." He gave her a quick kiss. "And we can't think about any of that now. We have to focus on what needs to be done. Push everything else out of your mind."

"Last time almost killed us," Maura whispered.

"But it didn't. We're here."

Maura knew Curtis was trying to sound reassuring, but they were in an impossible situation.

"Promise me," she whispered. "If ya have the chance to stop Buford, you'll take it no matter what else is happening. That is the only thing that matters. Nothing else. We end all of this tonight no matter the cost."

She saw by his expression that he understood what she was saying. If it became a choice of saving her or ending Buford, she wanted him to choose killing the vampire.

Maura should have done it herself when she had the chance. But she hadn't been able to make that sacrifice. She couldn't sacrifice Curtis. If it came down to it again, she didn't know what she would do.

"There is no point in living if you're not with me," he answered. "We go in together. We come out together."

"But we can't be selfish." Maura wrapped her arms around his neck. "My family."

"We go in together. We come out together," he repeated more firmly. "Say it."

Maura pulled back to study his expression.

"Say it," he demanded.

"We go in together. We come out together," Maura managed weakly.

"Good." Curtis took the lead, moving behind the cabins to hide within the shadows. They found a dirt road worn into the ground that led through what would have been a beautifully sculpted canopy of trees. All that remained were barren limbs left to rot after Maura had pulled the life from them to fuel her attack on the army.

They kept a quick pace, hurrying through the trees. The house appeared as if designed to invoke feelings of awe at its sudden appearance around a bend. It stood, pristine against the rustic setting of dead forest.

Torches had been lit in the yard, and lights shone from within the plantation house's windows. Maura glanced to where the vampire army had died. Marks scorched the yards though it appeared as if little tufts of grass had survived.

"Do ya think he's in there?" Maura asked.

Curtis nodded. "Vampires are close. I can feel it."

"I'd say let's wait for daylight and take them out when they sleep, but—"

"We're never here when daylight comes," he finished.

Maura tried to sense a way to fuel her magick, but there wasn't much nature left to power her.

They quickened their pace, sprinting over the open yard to the house only to press against the siding. As if by mutual agreement, they didn't speak but merely gestured. Maura went to a window and peeked through the slit in the curtain. She watched a housekeeper carry a stack of linens and disappear around a corner. From what she could tell of the couches and chairs, the home was exactly what she would have expected of a wealthy landowner pre-Civil War.

Another woman sat in one of the ridiculously uncomfortable gowns ladies of the time favored with a corset and hoop skirt. Only she clearly wasn't a lady. The ill-fitted material hung on her thin frame as if she'd been dressed up and deposited on the couch like a decoration. She appeared uncomfortable as she worried her hands in her lap.

Maura motioned toward the next window. Curtis went to peek inside. He searched the room before shaking his head. They ducked under the window and went to the next one, then around the corner to the next.

"I don't see them, but I can feel they're close," Curtis whispered.

Maura gripped her stake tight. They crept along the back of the house to keep checking inside.

Suddenly, cold hands grabbed her arms from behind. She was dragged backward, around the side of the house and over the front yard. Her heels created ruts in the earth as she tried to kick her way free.

"Curtis!" she yelled, gripping her stake tight so she wouldn't lose it.

"Maura, I'm coming!"

She heard Curtis running after her but only caught a glimpse of him during her struggle.

Virgile suddenly stopped dragging and sniffed at her neck. "How? He turned you. I saw it."

"Let. Me." Maura jerked violently to be free. She held onto the stake for dear life. "Go!"

"Maura, I'm—" Curtis tried to reach her, but Buford snatched him from above.

Maura cried out and fought harder. Buford hauled Curtis onto the roof and dropped him where she couldn't see.

"Curtis!" Maura had known they were up against great odds, but she'd thought they'd at least have a chance at a fight. This could not be how fate wanted their story to end.

But then, fate was often cruel.

Chapter Thirteen

Curtis felt the stake rolling out of his grasp but could not form a fist to stop it. The air had been knocked out of him when Buford flung him back first onto the rooftop. The clay shingles had cracked beneath him at the force. Cold air whistled around him, but it took several attempts before he could wheeze it into his lungs.

The vampire stood over him as if the elements and height didn't matter. And to him, it didn't. His hair blew wildly around his head, and his milky eyes stared with what could have been curiosity or disdain.

"How do you come to be here?" Buford asked. "Like this."

If Curtis could have talked over gasps for air, he would have told him that was a very complicated supernatural question for which he had little answers.

Honestly, he would probably just tell him to go fuck himself.

"You're it, aren't you? The child that was stolen a week past from my property. That's why you taste of my blood." Buford bent at the waist and looked him over. "How did you grow so fast? Was it the warlock? Did she cast a spell? Did those cheating wizards send her after they took my money and failed to deliver the prophecy they promised?"

Curtis realized the vampire thought he was Hazel's baby. He wondered if the vampire could feel anything toward his child or if being a father would affect him at all. Having known Buford in another time, he had his answer. Benign neglect was the best thing he'd ever done for his daughter.

Buford kneeled on the rook and swiped a long fingernail to cut Curtis's cheek. He spread the blood with his fingertip and then drew it under his nose to sniff.

Knowing what his blood had done to save Maura of the virus, he offered his neck and dared, "Go ahead. Take a bite. Try some."

The tip of Buford's finger began to smoke. The vampire quickly swiped it clean on Curtis's shirt. Seeing the reaction, Curtis smeared his fingers against his cheek wound and whacked Buford on the neck. The vampire screeched and recoiled as the blood made his skin bubble. Buford slapped at his face and neck to stop the burn.

"What's the matter? I thought you liked blood!" Curtis used the moment to find his footing.

Curtis looked for the stake and found it trapped against one of the clay shingles. He ran to pick up the weapon. When he tried to hold it, his dominant hand had trouble making a tight fist. He must have injured it when he hit the roof. Curtis was forced to carry the weapon in his left hand.

He heard Maura screaming as the faint sound came from below. The wind cut against him, making it difficult to hear. Curtis wished he could fly so that he could jump off the roof to save her.

"If ya have the chance to stop Buford, you'll take it no matter what else is happening. That is the only thing that matters. Nothing else. We end all of this tonight no matter the cost."

He knew what she would want him to do and why. Over a century from now, Buford would massacre her family unless they stopped him. For that reason alone, he would fight the urge to climb down by any means to get to Maura and remain on the roof to fight.

"We go in together. We come out together," he

whispered, hoping that in some way she would feel those words too and find a way to stay alive.

"Tell me how she did it," Buford demanded. "Tell me how she changed."

"She didn't do anything to me. I just grew up." Curtis hoped to keep Buford talking so he could get close enough to strike. He heaved for breath, and his heart pounded violently. Adrenaline flowed through him, blocking out any pain he should be feeling.

"Not you. Her. I gave her my mark. How did she stop from turning after you took her?" Buford asked. "No magick should be able to stop the vampiric gift once it's been bestowed."

Curtis thought of the scars along his chest and back. He'd be very aware for each one, and his agony mixed with his blood had saved her. He'd live through it a thousand times if it meant having one more moment with her. "Guess it wasn't magick then."

Buford circled him, forcing him to turn around. Curtis rubbed his hand against his bloody cheek. He'd take any advantage he could get.

"Doesn't matter. I plan to do it again. Only, this time, you won't be around to save her."

Chapter Fourteen

Maura's magick pulled energy from her surroundings. The grass tufts in the yard withered around her. It wasn't enough. Next, it tried to take from the women inside the house. Maura resisted the urge. She felt their weakened state. None of them had the energy to spare.

Maura gripped her stake tight and tried to swing her arm back to stab Virgile in the thigh. He shifted his weight, flinging her around. She couldn't reach him, and he was too strong for her to overpower him physically.

Curtis cried out in pain. The sound of his voice rained down over her from the rooftop. Maura struggled harder.

Virgile laughed. "Don't worry. The sire will dispose of your lover soon enough and come to claim you. This time you won't be escaping his bite."

Maura managed to stomp on his foot.

"Watch it," Virgile warned, though he appeared to be enjoying himself. "You're going to want to be nice to your new general."

"Fuck off, General Asshat," Maura answered. "I'll never follow ya."

Her magick searched desperately for a power source.

Virgile laughed. "Nothing to feed that magick of yours, witch?"

"I'm a warlock," Maura corrected, "ya ignorant piece of—"

"You don't have to be conscious for the sire to change you, just barely alive," Virgile growled, spinning her to face him. He bared his fangs, ready to bite.

Maura used all the strength and magick she had to thrust the stake at the vampire's heart. His teeth bit into her flesh, clamping on her shoulder. The stake tip sunk into his body. She threw herself toward him, using her weight to force the weapon in deep. The blunt edge became wedged against her collarbone.

Virgile's screeched in surprise. His mouth unlatched, and he fell back onto the ground but not before grabbing hold of her wrist. His free hand circled the stake protruding from his chest, trying to pull it out as the other held on tight.

Maura tugged at her arm to free herself, but she'd used up all her strength on that one blow. She tried to kick at his arm but kept missing.

The vampire's flesh began to darken as he burned from the inside out. High-pitched screeches wailed over the countryside. Maura covered one ear as the sound rattled her to the bone. The heat of his body burned her wrist, and she shrieked in pain. Virgile's skin cracked, and the death fire erupted from within his body. The flames charred the stake.

Maura finally broke free when his wrist broke away from the rest of him. She pried his fingers from her seared wrist.

Maura stumbled backward toward the house, watching to make sure Virgile disappeared from the earth forever. The vampire struggled until the breeze blew the very last smidgen of ash from his body into oblivion.

Maura clutched her injured hand and sprinted toward the house. She glanced up, not able to see what was happening on the roof.

She burst through the front door. The thick wood slammed open with a reverberating thump. Two human maids gaped in fright at her entrance. They clung to each other. Fresh bitemarks littered their arms and chest. At Maura's attention, they ran in the opposite direction.

Maura darted to the stairs, desperate to find a way onto the roof. She took them two at a time. When she reached the landing, she began flinging open doors. Finally seeing the bedroom window, she ran to it. The ground was a straight drop from the second story, but she didn't care.

Footsteps ran the length of the bedroom ceiling, followed by several loud thuds. They were still there, fighting.

Maura grabbed a pillow from the bed and used it to pad her fist as she punched the glass. The panes shattered and fell to the ground below. She then kicked at the wood frame.

Blood trickled down her arm from where Virgile bit her. Her chest ached where the end of the stake rammed against her. The forming bruise weakened her shoulder.

"Curtis," she yelled to let him know she was near. "Curtis, I'm coming. We go in together. We come out together!"

Maura swiped her hand dry before climbing onto the narrow ledge. Her magick had been depleted, and it was by sheer will that she managed to pull and kick and climb her way up to the roof's ledge. She dug her toes into the siding for leverage and swung her leg. Her foot slipped, and she almost fell. She didn't give herself time to think of the long drop down as she tried it again.

Maura fought and clawed her way over the edge. Her legs dangled over the side as her stomach pressed to the rooftop. She allowed several deep, ragged breaths before hooking her knee over the top to wiggle her way onto the flat roof's surface.

She'd made it.

Maura's heart felt like it would beat its way out of her chest while the matching pulse kept time in her neck. Her fatigued muscles trembled, and they didn't want to listen to her commands as she tried to push herself to her feet.

Maura saw the two figures struggling on the opposite side of the roof. She managed a low crawl toward them. Curtis punched Buford in the face and stomach. The vampire laughed, barely affected.

Curtis charged, yelling in a fit of violence. Buford sidestepped with supernatural speed and shoved Curtis onto his back. The sound of Buford's taunting laughter continued to ring.

Seeing Curtis gave her newfound strength. Maura's limbs continued to shake as she forced herself to stand. The wind was much stronger at this height, and she held up her arm to block it from her eyes as she charged forward to help.

Buford's attention turned toward her, and he started to smile. Curtis used the vampire's moment of distraction to spring to his feet. He rammed Buford in the stomach before Maura could reach them. The two men collided in an ugly thud before falling off the roof. They disappeared over the side.

"Curtis!" Maura tripped as she scrambled to the edge. She reached down, hoping beyond reason to catch him, all the while knowing she was too late.

Maura peered over the side of the roof in time to see a great burst of flames coming from the ground. The vampire bonfire was much more prominent than Virgile's, burning brighter and hotter.

Curtis had done it. Buford was dead.

Maura held herself locked in that terrible moment between hope and despair. When the ash of Buford's body finally blew away, Curtis lay on the ground below, his leg and arm bent at broken angles. His eyes stared toward the sky but didn't move to look at her.

Maura kept her arm over the side, her grasping fingers reaching down as if she could will him to come to her. He didn't move. She used her magick to see if it detected any life left in him.

Nothing.

Curtis was dead.

Maura felt the emptiness of that loss. They had accomplished what they set out to do. The vampires were dead, and the future would be saved if such a thing were possible. She stared at Curtis's body and suddenly realized if they didn't go back, then maybe the future would have to be erased. Perhaps this is the way their story was always supposed to end.

Maura cried out, so very tired from the battle. All her magick was used up, and her heart was broken, leaving her an empty vessel. She had traveled through time with him, and though their moment had been too brief, she had loved him enough for infinite lifetimes. Wherever he was going to next, that is where she would go too.

Maura pushed to her hands and knees, unable to make it to her feet. With only the thought of being with him in her head, she flung herself off the roof headfirst.

Chapter Fifteen

Maura stood on the sidewalk outside of her motel. The air had a strange energy to it, like the threat of a coming storm. When she'd gone inside, the sky had been clear. Now clouds cast shadows in the moonlight. She wondered if her cousins were messing with the weather again. Erik was particularly talented at controlling the wind.

Her scalp tingled from a static electrical charge, and she felt her hair lifting. Maura smoothed it down. The sound of battle drums came from one of the guest rooms, and she frowned. The other guests would start calling to complain about the noise soon.

As if to prove her point, the phone in the lobby began to ring. Maura followed the sound of the drums. Seeing the flash of a television screen through the curtains, she pressed her ear to the door and listened to the Civil War documentary. A chill worked over her, and she had a feeling of déjà vu.

Maura knocked firmly on the door and waited. A burly man in boxer shorts answered, holding a beer. He frowned in annoyance.

"You're not pizza," he said.

"Hi. I'm Maura from the front desk. We're going to need to ask ya to turn your television down. We're receiving noise complaints from the other guests."

The man looked put out and sighed heavily. "Yeah, yeah, all right."

He rudely closed the door on her.

"Thank ya!" she called, trying to put a smile in her voice even though she was annoyed by his attitude. Such was the life of customer service.

Maura waited for the television volume to go down before walking back toward the lobby. Her steps slowed as she again looked at the sky. The slight change in the atmosphere would be ignored by most, but she'd lived long enough to know to trust her instincts. Something was off.

She watched the parking lot as an empty plastic bag blew between the cars. Tension filled her, and she had the strangest feeling that she needed to get ready for a fight.

"It's done," Bruce stated, strolling toward her.

"What?" Maura blinked, confused, startled by his approach.

"Medusa, Stheno, and Euryale are now beach ready," he answered.

"What?" Maura tried to follow what he was saying.

"I painted bikinis on the naked gorgons like ya asked." Bruce stopped next to her and studied her face with concern. "Are ya feeling all right? Did ya forget to eat again today?"

Maura started to shake her head and then frowned. Maybe that was what caused the grumpy, fighting feeling inside of her. "I don't remember."

"Ya can't keep doing this," Bruce scolded. "Come on. The Butlers aren't coming back. Let's light the No Vacancy sign and go get burgers."

"No. That's OK. Ya go. I should finish up some paperwork. Would ya mind just bringing me back something?" Maura made a move to go back inside the lobby.

"Stop," Bruce ordered. She saw his reflection on the glass door. He twirled his finger toward the sign. The No Vacancy light came on. He nodded his head at the lobby door. She heard it latch shut. "Get in the car. Ya look like you're about to pass out. Plus, ya need a break. It's either get drive-thru with me, or I'm calling Ma to tell her ya are not taking care of yourself."

"Burgers sound awesome." Maura laughed, giving in to his threat.

The plastic bag caught her attention. That wasn't right. It wasn't supposed to be a bag.

"Ya know, Maura, there's something I've learned in my centuries of living." He slung his arm around her shoulders. "There's always more work and always more excuses not to live."

"I think that probably sounded more profound in your head." Maura walked around the side of Bruce's car and got in.

"Things usually do." He chuckled as he slid into the driver's seat. "Any requests?"

"Any drive-thru is fine. I don't care," Maura answered.

Bruce started to pull out of the parking lot when suddenly something pounded on the trunk of his car. They gasped in unison, turning to see what it was.

Naked Raibeart rushed to the passenger door. Maura rolled down her window.

"Move over," Raibeart said.

"Get in the back," she countered as she opened the door and leaned forward with the seat so he could climb into the vehicle.

"There should be an extra kilt in the bag behind my seat," Bruce said.

"Drive, laddie!" Raibeart pounded the back of Bruce's seat to relay his urgency.

"Did ya rob a bank?" Maura teased, not returning his sense of panic.

"Ya need to find another accomplice. I'll not be Clyde to your Bonnie," Bruce added, crossing his arms over his chest as he grinned at his sister.

"They're coming!" Raibeart banged his fist again while kicking Bruce in the back of his seat.

"Who is—?" Bruce began.

"Gremians!" Raibeart shouted, pointing through the windshield. A knobby little creature leaped onto the hood and began pounding the window. The gnarled pests were a reasonably harmless nuisance. At worst, they scratched and disassembled light fixtures.

"What did ya do?" Maura watched the gremian fling itself at the window. Was this the fight she had felt coming? She suppressed a laugh. Thankfully human motel guests would not be able to see it.

"I might have proposed to her. But to be fair, I was drunk at the time, and she looked different," Raibeart said.

"Oh, in that case, maybe we should let our

new aunt into the car." Bruce reached to roll down the window.

Raibeart waved his hand and forced the car to accelerate. Since Bruce had already put the vehicle into reverse when Raibeart stopped them, he had to navigate backward through the parking lot quickly.

"All right, stop!" Bruce yelled as he fought to regain control of the car. "I'll drive."

Raibeart watched them outpace the creature before sitting back in his seat. "So, youngsters, where we are going?"

"Drive-thru," Bruce answered.

"How about we stop by a liquor store and go into the pizza buffet? I could use a drink," Raibeart said.

"The pizzeria has a dress code." Maura pointed behind her head toward the floor. "As in, ya have to be dressed to go inside."

"Oh, aye, bloody prudes." Raibeart dug through the bag, and she could hear him putting on clothes.

Chapter Sixteen

Curtis threw the trash bag into the dumpster and sighed as he looked up at the sky. The sound of country music drifted from the back door of Crimson Tavern as it hung open. It was nights like this that he missed home.

He'd talked to his mawmaw earlier about moving back home. Things in Green Vallis were not going as he'd hoped. Maybe following "signs" and buying a place on a whim hadn't been the most brilliant move. The restaurant had customers, but not enough to make the kind of financial difference that he'd hoped, and he could own a restaurant in the Mississippi Delta just as easily. At least there he'd be by friends and family.

Curtis never planned on marrying unless he happened to find companionship with a barren woman. He didn't want to risk passing his dhampir blood to a new generation. Even though the demon vampire who'd sired his mawmaw and his undead army had died in an epic battle against two angels, or so the family legend went, that evil blood lived on in him. Mortal women who became pregnant with dhampir children didn't live through childbirth. The babies sucked the life out of them, as Curtis had sucked the life out of his mother. His father had tried, but when Curtis was a teenager, he'd hung himself in the garage.

There weren't many dhampirs in the world for a reason. They were the bastard children of evil. He felt that monster inside him every time someone else's blood touched his skin. He wouldn't turn into a vampire, but the rage would stir until he couldn't control his actions. Curtis had spent a lifetime learning to relax and control his temper.

Curtis went back inside, stopping by the sink to wash his hands. Burgers sizzled on the grill.

Kay popped her head into the kitchen. "Hey, boss, it's still OK that I take off right at close tonight, right?"

Years of smoking had left Kay's voice with a gravelly sound. She was a decent waitress and remembered her orders but swore in front of customers and took a lot of smoke breaks.

"Yeah, that's fine." Curtis placed the burgers on the buns already awaiting in the to-go containers. He debated on how soon he should tell her his plan to close.

Maybe later. He needed to sort out a buyer first.

"You're the best." Kay grinned. "I think I saw a car heading this way when I was out on my break just now. Want me to take the order?"

"Naw, I'll take care of it." He closed the container lids. "Here's the to-go order. You can take off as soon as you drop checks at your tables. I'll put the tips in your envelope and watch them until they leave."

"Mm, love you!" Kay said. "If you weren't my boss, I'd kiss you."

Curtis smiled, knowing she meant no such thing. Kay tended to sound like she came on to everyone. It's probably why so many of the older male clients requested to be in her section.

When he was again alone, he took a deep breath and leaned against the prep table. Maybe those MacGregors would be interested in purchasing this place. They had been taking over a lot of the local businesses. With luck, he could go back with a little bit of money in his pocket to open a new restaurant.

Curtis remained torn. He had been so sure he

was meant to be here and that Wisconsin held something special for him. He laughed at his naivety. It was probably the ley lines beneath the town that had tricked him, pied-pipering him like it did so many supernatural beings.

It was too bad. He liked the town. It would have been great if the business supported him staying.

He felt as if he'd come to the end of a long journey. Maybe he'd done what he needed to do in Green Vallis and didn't realize it. Maybe him giving Kay a job and saving her from foreclosure had been enough of a reason. And now, it was his time to go home.

Chapter Seventeen

Bruce sped through the streets a little too fast.

"How was I supposed to know I was still banned from the pizzeria," Raibeart protested from the back seat.

"Ya proposed to the man's wife," Bruce reasoned. "I don't think there is a statute of limitation on that one."

"She told me she was single," Raibeart said. "I don't mess with married women. That bond is sacred."

"Evidently not to her." Bruce slowed as they neared Main Street but rolled through the stop sign. There wasn't much downtown traffic on weeknights. "That's all right. This place has better food. We'll try to catch them before they close."

Maura just wanted to go back to the motel,

snarf down a greasy triple patty hamburger in private, take a bath, and go to bed. What was supposed to be a quick run through a drive-thru had turned into a family dinner.

The old-fashioned tavern sign hung over the sidewalk, reading, "Crimson Tavern." She'd only been inside the building a couple of times, but the place had stirred a sense of nostalgia in the MacGregor family. It reminded them of the old taverns, from a time they'd arrive by horseback and drink sour ale to cover the taste of the questionable food. That's about where the nostalgia ended. Sure, there were wooden floors and tables and a smattering of historical decorations, but also neon signs and flat-screen televisions. The most significant difference between this tavern and the past was this restaurant's food was hands down some of the best she'd ever had in her life.

Less than a dozen locals sat in the booths but looked to be finishing up their meals. Low country music played over the speakers. A table of three women waved as Bruce and Raibeart entered. The MacGregor men had a way of hamming up the local celebrity angle. It had everything to do with accents and kilts.

"Ladies," Raibeart waved back, and the forty-something friends laughed.

"Your kilt is on backward," Bruce stated, striding past his uncle.

Raibeart glanced down. "That's the fashion."

Bruce made his way to a table in the back, grabbing menus along the way. Maura sat down next to her brother. Raibeart had detoured to talk to the women.

"Which one do ya think will be our new aunt?" Maura studied the three choices.

Bruce studied the menu. "My money is on the gremian."

"How's it going tonight? Can I start you off with some drinks?" A man with a soft Southern accent appeared beside the table. Maura glanced up, smiling at him. He had a friendly face, trustworthy. There was a paranormal vibe about him, and she tried to remember if her cousins had ever mentioned a supernatural working at the tavern.

"Hey, Curtis, good to see ya again," Bruce said. Her brother didn't appear to be concerned about the supernatural element. "We're not too late to order, are we?"

"You just made it. We normally close in fifteen, but I haven't shut down the grills yet. Kay's ending her shift, so I'll be taking care of you," Curtis answered.

The waitress came from the back kitchen carrying two check holders.

"Nice, thanks." Bruce set the menu down. "We'll keep it simple. Three burgers, two fries, one kettle chips, and whatever's on tap."

"Loaded tater tot nachos," Maura added. She couldn't help staring at his handsome face. There was something about him.

"Local favorite." Curtis smiled at her attention. He held a notepad but didn't bother to write any of it down.

Maura quickly averted her gaze and pretended to look at a dessert menu. What in the hell was wrong with her?

"MacGregor family favorite," Bruce corrected.

"Coming right up." Curtis dropped his order pad into his apron and started to turn. He stopped himself and then turned back to Maura. "You know, every time I think I've met all of you, more show up." Curtis held out his hand. "Curtis Jefferson."

"Oh, sorry. I didn't realize ya two hadn't met. This is my sister." Bruce took her dessert menu from her to free up her hands.

"Maura." She smiled, reaching for him. "MacGregor, obviously."

"Curtis owns this joint," Bruce said.

Curtis's hand grasped hers, and she felt a jolt of lightning run through her. A rush of images filled her mind, bizarre things she'd only seen in dreams—rivers of blood, marching ghosts, horrible scars, battles that had never happened…

Or had they?

Fuzzy pieces became clear as they fell into place. She'd met this man before, on many occasions, in many ways. They had fought battles and lost. They'd traveled through time, saved lives, lost those same lives. They'd helped a woman give birth. Sometimes the baby lived, and sometimes it died. They'd fought. They'd made love. They'd died in each other's arms. They'd fallen in love so many times. They'd also fallen apart.

And once, they'd won.

She remembered plummeting to her death toward his broken body from a rooftop to be with him. The heartbreak surfaced only to be repaired instantly now that he was alive.

"Maura?" Bruce touched her arm. "What is it?"

Maura gasped, drawing her hand away from Curtis. She searched his now-familiar face. Emotions rushed through her as she tried to make sense of all the timelines she was seeing. She pushed up from her seat.

"I love ya," she stated.

"Whoa, sis, easy, they're just nachos," Bruce said. "I'm sorry, low blood sugar. She hasn't eaten—"

"I love you, too," Curtis answered, pulling her into his arms. He kissed her hard. An eternity of pain and longing was in his embrace.

"Um, ah, Maura?" Bruce insisted. "Did Raibeart slip ya something? You're starting to worry me."

Maura ignored her brother.

"About time. I thought ya two lost souls were going to keep looping for an eternity," Raibeart said. Maura stiffened in surprise when her uncle bear-hugged the both of them together. "It's good to see ya kids finally have it sorted out."

Raibeart released them, giving two hearty pats on their backs before taking Maura's seat as his own.

"Ya know what's happening?" Bruce asked, confused.

Maura barely paid attention to them. She stared at Curtis in amazement. He was everything she ever wanted out of life.

"Ya silly children." Raibeart shook his head and laughed to himself. "Ya should take a page out of my romance book. I keep things easy, simple. None of this twenty time loops to get it right nonsense. Jefferson. Curtis. Jefferson. Curtis." He waved his hand in dismissal. "Half the time, I can never remember what ya call yourself."

"Curtis," Curtis stated.

"This time around," Raibeart mumbled. Suddenly, he frowned. "Och, no!"

"What?" Bruce asked.

"This means I won't get to play with my little Abigail again," Raibeart answered. "She's a sweet wee bairn. Loves her Uncle Raibeart and Cousin Jewel."

"You know my grandmother?" Curtis asked.

"Aye," Raibeart said.

He stared at him for a moment, then nodded. "That's right. You took care of her all those times we…"

"Yeah, I remember that too." Maura pulled him toward the bar, away from Raibeart's distracting. "This morning was just normal. I can't believe…"

"This is…"

"Yes." Maura nodded. "We won. We finally won."

"How many times did we try?"

"Twenty? Thirty?" Maura rubbed her temple. "It's a bit of a blur. The one thing I remember is, I love ya. I never want to be without ya. I've waited so long to say those words to ya."

"I love you, and I want to marry you. I never want us to be apart again." Curtis leaned in to kiss her but was interrupted by a shout.

"Hey, Jennifer, how've you been?" Kay called. Maura glanced over to see Rory and Jennifer enter the restaurant. They made a beeline straight for Bruce's table.

Maura turned back to Curtis. "I'm sorry, ya were saying?"

"Marry me," he stated.

Maura held him tighter. "Yes, of course."

Curtis held her tight and kissed her. People started to clap and cheer.

"Drinks on the house!" Kay yelled.

"Why's your sister making out with tavern guy?" Rory asked Bruce, his voice purposefully loud.

"That's *your* sister," Bruce countered.

"Because," Jennifer answered her husband, "I told you. Those nachos are life changing."

Chapter Eighteen

EPILOGUE

Maura watched as Curtis pulled his car into the Hotel Motel parking lot. He'd just picked his mawmaw up from the airport so Maura could finally meet the adult Abigail in person. From what Curtis had told her, Abigail had lived an extraordinary life mainly spent in service to helping others.

Curtis had moved into the motel with Maura. As an engagement gift, Bruce had painted cartoon soldiers on their walls, hiding behind a forest of trees as a joke. Neither Curtis nor Maura found the design very funny. Unfortunately, the paint was enchanted and would take time to fade.

Bruce was inside the lobby watching the front desk, which pretty much meant reading a book and letting customer calls go to voicemail. Maura was too excited to care. She knew how much Abigail meant to Curtis, and he had missed seeing her.

It had taken several weeks, but the memories of all they'd gone through together had come into sharper focus. Though the details of the magick that caused the time loops were unclear, they determined Jewel had something to do with it. She was one of a very short list of creatures powerful enough to make it happen. When Buford attacked the first time, there had been no time travel or Abigail. Jewel's self-preservation had caused her magick to surge. She was too young to focus it, so it became a messy loop of time, restarting over and over again until they found the right outcome.

For some reason, Raibeart was the only other family member who could remember living through every one of the time loops. No one was sure why, except that Raibeart generally didn't see things the way other people did. He was also constantly with Jewel, protecting her.

The rest of the family drew a complete blank and recalled nothing. Since Maura had watched them die on several occasions, she was glad they didn't remember.

Maura gave a little bounce of excitement as Curtis parked the car in front of her and got out.

She saw Abigail through the front windshield. The older woman smiled and waved as Curtis ran around the car to open her door for her. Wrinkles lined her face, adding character more than acting as a testament to her age.

Maura felt someone standing next to her and turned to see Raibeart in a clown costume. "What the…?"

Her uncle held a handful of tulips in his puffy-gloved hand. When Abigail's door shut, Raibeart stepped in front of Maura to block her as he went in for a hug.

"Raibeart!" Maura rushed after him, but it was too late.

"Oh," Abigail gasped in surprise. "Well, hello there."

"Abby, my sweet wee bairn." Raibeart continued to hold her.

Abigail patted his arms and looked caught between surprise and amusement.

"Ya look the same as when they took ya away from me," Raibeart said. "I thought I'd never see ya again. How have ya been, love?"

"Raibeart, it's only been a month for ya," Maura scolded. And, according to her uncle's timeline, that was the truth. He'd been with baby Abigail. For the adult Abigail, it would have been more like one-hundred-and-sixty-plus years, give or take.

"Ya can't understand the breaking of a parent's heart until ya are one," Raibeart scolded as he released Abigail to gaze lovingly at her. Tears streamed down his face.

"You're right, Uncle Raibeart. I'm sorry." Maura smiled and patted Raibeart's shoulder. The man had taken care of Abigail during many of the time loops.

"You know, most people are scared of them, but I've always been rather fond of clowns." Abigail lightly honked Raibeart's nose and laughed.

Curtis leaned into Maura for a quick kiss. "I missed you."

"We need to talk later," she answered.

He looked somewhat concerned but nodded.

"Mawmaw," Curtis went to rescue his grand-mother from Raibeart's fawning. He guided her gently by the elbow. "I'd like you to meet my fiancée, Maura MacGregor."

Raibeart had tears streaming down his painted face. He clutched his puffy hands over his heart. The tulips had fallen to the ground in his excitement.

"Maura!" Abigail held her arms wide for a

hug. "Come here, girl. I'm so delighted to put a beautiful face to the voice on the phone."

"We are so happy to have ya here with us, Abigail," Maura said, returning the hug.

"Oh, that's Mawmaw to you," Abigail said. "After all, you're family now."

"Mawmaw," Maura agreed, letting the woman go.

"I told Mawmaw that she's welcome to stay here as long as she likes," Curtis said. "Forever even."

"Yes, our home is your home." Maura gestured to the motel and laughed. "As ya can see, you'd have your pick of rooms."

Curtis went to the car to get the suitcases.

Abigail laughed and leaned closer to Maura. "Curtis tells me your brother painted a Tarzan room."

Maura checked her surprise before it showed and nodded. "Uh, yeah, do ya want that room?"

Abigail winked and nodded.

"You're welcome to wait inside the lobby while we get your suitcases," Maura offered.

"Hey, Abby," Raibeart said. "Do ya happen to remember the bear party?"

"No." Abigail took up Raibeart's extended arm and let him escort her into the motel lobby. "You know, you do seem awfully familiar, Mr. Clown, but I'm having a hard time placing you exactly. Maybe you should remind me about this bear party."

Maura joined Curtis by the trunk and grabbed the smaller of Abigail's two suitcases. "I have been dying to tell ya something."

"You're going to put my mawmaw in a room that has a half-naked man in a leaf loincloth painted on the wall?" He chuckled.

"Well, yeah, what Mawmaw wants, she gets." Maura grinned. She couldn't help it. Happiness bubbled out of her, unable to be contained. "But also, I went by the mansion today to talk to my ma about something."

"Oh, yeah? Everything OK there?" He closed the trunk and put his keys into his pocket.

Maura placed the smaller suitcase on the ground and reached for his hand. "It turns out it wasn't bad shellfish. I'm pregnant."

A wave of fear passed over his expression, and he dropped the suitcase he held.

"Relax, love," she cupped his face in her hands. "I'm not human. My ma said I'll be fine. Maybe we'll need a couple of spells to help me along, but this is a good thing."

He gave a stunned nod of his head. "Oh, my... You're..."

Maura grinned. "Pregnant."

He took a deep breath.

Her smile fell some. "Tell me what you're thinking because I think there is nothing more wonderful than a piece of you and me together creating life."

"I'm a dhampir."

"And ya didn't turn out half bad. I know you're nervous, but all new parents have something they worry about." She gave a meaningful glance toward where Abigail was in the lobby. "In fact, every dhampir I have ever met is wonderful."

He nodded but his expression only became more concerned.

"What else?" she asked.

"I'm thinking I don't know how to change a diaper," he said, smiling cautiously. "And we're going to need supplies. I don't have supplies. There are knives in the kitchen."

Maura laughed and wrapped her arms around him. "You're forgetting something."

"What? Oh, I love you."

"Well, that, aye, I love you too. But also, you're marrying into the MacGregor family. We won't have to change diapers. That's what the elders are for."

Curtis slowly smiled and began to relax. "Raibeart did do a great job with Abigail."

"He did."

He nodded. "OK, yeah, a baby."

Curtis made a soft noise as he kissed her. His hand strayed to her stomach. Whispering against her lips, he said, "I never thought I would find such happiness. Thank you for everything, my sweet Maura MacGregor."

"I love you," she answered. The breeze shifted, and the day felt perfect. Things were just as they should be in Green Vallis.

The End

The Series Continues

WARLOCKS MACGREGOR® 10: A STREAK OF LIGHTNING

Ladies, watch out! Raibeart MacGregor is on the prowl and looking for his true love. He has only one question for you lassies, "Will ya marry me?"

Magic, Mischief and Kilts!

From the Highlands of Scotland to the valleys of Wisconsin... A modern-day Scottish paranormal romance by NYT Bestselling Author Michelle M. Pillow.

Warning: Contains yummy, hot, mischievous MacGregors who are almost certainly up to no good on their quest to find true love. And Uncle Raibeart.

Warlocks MacGregor® Series

SCOTTISH MAGICKAL WARLOCKS

Love Potions
Spellbound
Stirring Up Trouble
Cauldrons and Confessions
Spirits and Spells
Kisses and Curses
Magick and Mischief
A Dash of Destiny
Night Magick
A Streak of Lightning
Magickal Trouble

More Coming Soon

Visit www.MichellePillow.com for details.

Newsletter

To stay informed about when a new book in the series installments is released, sign up for updates:

Sign up for Michelle's Newsletter
michellepillow.com/author-updates

About Michelle M. Pillow

New York Times **& USA TODAY**
Bestselling Author

Michelle loves to travel and try new things, whether it's a paranormal investigation of an old Vaudeville Theatre or climbing Mayan temples in Belize. She believes life is an adventure fueled by copious amounts of coffee.

Newly relocated to the American South, Michelle is involved in various film and documentary projects with her talented director husband. She is mom to a fantastic artist. And she's managed by a dog and cat who make sure she's meeting her deadlines.

For the most part she can be found wearing pajama pants and working in her office. There may or may not be dancing. It's all part of the creative process.

Come say hello! Michelle loves talking with readers on social media!

www.MichellePillow.com

facebook.com/AuthorMichellePillow

twitter.com/michellepillow

instagram.com/michellempillow

bookbub.com/authors/michelle-m-pillow

goodreads.com/Michelle_Pillow

amazon.com/author/michellepillow

youtube.com/michellepillow

pinterest.com/michellepillow

Complimentary Material

Second Chance Magic

BY MICHELLE M. PILLOW

Order of Magic Book One
by Michelle M. Pillow

Secrets broke her heart... and have now come back from the grave to haunt her.

So far, Lorna Addams' forties are not what she expected. After a very public embarrassment, she finds it difficult to trust her judgment when it comes to new friendships and dating. She might be willing to give love a second chance when she meets the attractive William Warrick, if only she could come to terms with what her husband did to her and leave it in the past.

How is a humiliated empty nest widow supposed to move on with her life? It's not like she can develop a sixth sense, séance her ex back, force him to tell her why and give her closure. Or can she?

Second Chance Magic Excerpt

This was not where Lorna Addams wanted to be. Tears filled her eyes and she was afraid to look down, so instead she stared at a flower arrangement. Her hand rested on top of satin and the smooth texture slid against the wood underneath.

"I'm sorry for your loss."

Lorna nodded, not seeing who spoke. She wished people would stop saying that. They meant well, but she didn't want to hear it.

At the sound of murmuring voices, she turned toward the gathering crowd. The funeral home continued to fill as people came to pay their respects to her dead husband. She only recognized about half of them but assumed the expensively dressed men and women knew Glenn from work. Her husband had a few nice suits but he wasn't— *hadn't been*—pretentious. Not like this crowd. He had liked to keep his home life away from his job. He called his family his oasis.

Why were these people even invited? If Lorna

had been in charge of the arrangements and not a trustee, she would have kept the event for family and close friends only.

"I'm so sorry for your loss." Jackie, her cousin, forced a hug on her. Lorna stood still, letting it happen as she counted the seconds until she was released.

Over Jackie's shoulder, Lorna glanced toward the front row of seats where Nicholas, Jacob, and Jennifer huddled together. Though they were all technically adults, they'd always be her babies. Jennifer's dark head rested against her twin's shoulder, trembling as Jacob tried to comfort her. It broke Lorna's heart to see her strong daughter brought to such sorrow. Jacob's lips were pressed tight and he had been staring at the same spot on the floor for nearly an hour. The two had always been close. They even planned on starting at the same college in the fall.

Nicholas, the oldest, looked the most like his father, reminding Lorna of when she'd first met Glenn. He was almost finished with his under-graduate degree in accounting. He should have been at his summer internship, not here. None of them should have been here.

Jackie finally let go as she made a bit of a scene, gasping and sobbing. Lorna wanted to remind her cousin that they weren't close. Jackie barely knew Glenn. The last time they'd seen each other had been nearly five years ago at a family reunion.

Some people appeared to glide through life— an average family, quiet dramas, envious paths. Their struggles, though real to them, seemed small compared to those of the rest of the world. Their bads were never as bad, their goods consistent. They looked to have all the answers to happiness. That was Lorna's life before this day— perfectly uneventful, no made-for-TV-drama. In fact, for long stretches, she would have admitted her life was even dull.

She'd give anything for boring right now.

Lorna finally forced her gaze to the casket. The funeral director had tried to tell her it would look like Glenn was sleeping. It didn't.

Lorna frowned. Glenn's hair had been combed all wrong. He hated when his bangs were pulled forward. It matched a large portrait of her husband displayed near Glenn's head. Lorna had never seen the picture before. In fact, she'd never seen the suit they'd put on him. It wasn't the clothes she'd dropped off for him.

Glenn had appointed a trustee he'd met through work to take care of all his funeral arrangements. Honestly, Lorna had been grateful not to have to make any of the decisions. But then, she'd assumed the trustee would make sure everything was perfect.

She leaned forward to fix Glenn's hair, brushing it back. There was nothing she could do about the portrait. It looked like it belonged on an ID badge from the consulting firm Glenn worked at.

"How did you know my husband?"

Lorna turned at the strange question. Her mind was in a fog and it was possible she'd misheard. The woman who spoke looked like she'd stepped off a movie set in her tight black dress and large-brim black hat. A veil covered her face, making it hard to see all of the details.

Lorna glanced behind her to the chairs. She now recognized less than half the crowd. This lady clearly belonged with them. Who were these people? Lorna's dress was shabbier by comparison and had come off a department store sales rack years ago. She didn't have many reasons to wear black.

Lorna stared numbly as the woman leaned over to smooth Glenn's bangs down to match the photo. The large diamond of the lady's ring begged people to look at her hand like a shiny distraction. Lorna glanced at the plain band on her finger.

"Please, stop," Lorna tried to lift her hand, but

it didn't feel as if it belonged to her body. Nothing felt real. "He hates his hair like that."

The woman pulled the veil over her head, away from her face. Her makeup was perfect, including the thick black lines around her eyes. If Lorna had put on makeup, she would have cried it off long before now.

"How exactly did you know my husband?" the woman repeated, her tone annoyed as she directed a withering glare in Lorna's direction.

What was going on here? Was this a sick joke?

Glenn had been *her* husband for twenty years. These were *their* children sitting in the front row. This tightness in her chest was a wife's grief. This day was stressful enough and it was all she could do to stay upright. Who said such a thing to a grieving widow? Now? In front of the deceased's three children?

"That's not funny," Lorna whispered, not wanting to create a scene to upset her kids.

"Omigod, you're *her*, aren't you? That's why his funeral is in this dump of a town, and why the man handling the estate couldn't look me in the eye? Glenn just had to get one last dig at me. You have some nerve showing up here." This time the woman's voice was louder. "Leave now or I will have you thrown out."

"I don't know what your deal is, but——" Lorna

instantly stopped talking when Jacob appeared next to her.

"Mom, what's wrong?" Jacob took a protective stance in front of her. Lorna wasn't sure how to answer. To the other woman, he said, "I think you need to leave."

"What's going on here? Cheryl, are you all right?" One of the tailored gentlemen appeared next to the lady.

"No, Frank," Cheryl hissed. "I need you to get Glenn's mistress out of here before I scream. I can't take much more. I swear to God I can't."

Mistress? Lorna gasped at the insult. Jacob looked at her in confusion. Lorna wasn't sure what to say to her son. How could she explain whatever this was? She didn't understand it herself.

Cheryl reached into her small clutch and pulled out a cigarette from a metal case. Frank automatically retrieved a lighter from his suit jacket and lit it for her.

"Ma'am, you can't smoke in here." Mr. Wilkens, the owner of the funeral home, stepped forward to stop her.

Cheryl blew smoke in his direction. "Shut up or I'll have you fired. Can't you see I'm grieving?"

Mr. Wilkens glanced at Lorna in question but backed away from the hostile woman.

"This is my mom, and that is *her* husband and

my father," Jacob stated, his tone condescending enough to match the woman's. "I don't know what kind of scam you're trying to pull, lady, but it's you who needs to leave. I won't have you disrespecting my father's memory, and I sure as hell will not stand for you upsetting my mother."

"Father?" Cheryl swayed on her feet, eyeing Jacob. She waved her cigarette toward Frank who instantly took it from her fingers. He wrapped his arm around her waist to hold her upright. "Did you say *my* husband fathered…"

"He's our father. Not your husband." Jennifer appeared next to Jacob. She held her cellphone. To her twin, she said, "I'm calling the police."

Cheryl's eyes landed on Nicholas and she visibly stiffened.

"I think you should get your friend out of here, mister," Jacob said to Frank. "I don't know what kind of psychological issues she has going on, and I hope you get her help, but my parents have been happily married for twenty years."

"I've known Glenn since we were five. This is his wife, Cheryl. I think it's *you* who better go," Frank answered.

"That young man looks just like Glenn." Cheryl clutched Frank's arm as she continued to stare at Nicholas.

"We'll get this sorted, Cheryl," said Frank. "I'm sure it's not true."

Lorna saw everyone staring at them. The conversation had become loud and they were being watched like reality television. Her friends and family looked on in pity and confusion. The strangers in their suits and fancy dresses watched with disdain, some shaking their heads as if she'd done something wrong.

Under her breath, Cheryl said to Frank, "I don't care how many illegitimate bastards Glenn has, they're not getting a dime of my money."

"He's my husband," Lorna yelled. She'd had enough of this. "Mine!"

"Make them go away," Cheryl demanded just as loudly, "Get them out of here!"

"He's my…" A sharp pain erupted inside Lorna and she pressed her balled fist to her chest. At first she thought it was another wave of grief but, as she felt herself falling toward where Glenn's body lay in the casket, the world spun into blackness. She didn't try to fight it.

To find out more about Michelle's books visit www.MichellePillow.com

Please Leave a Review

Please take a moment to share your thoughts by reviewing this book.

Be sure to check out Michelle's other titles at www.MichellePillow.com